LOCADIO'S
APPRENTICE

LOCADIO'S APPRENTICE

CHELSEA QUINN YARBRO

HARPER & ROW
PUBLISHERS

For my friend
Larry Yep

Designed by Joyce Hopkins
1 2 3 4 5 6 7 8 9 10
FIRST EDITION

Library of Congress Cataloging in Publication Data
Yarbro, Chelsea Quinn, date
  Locadio's apprentice.

  Summary: A young Pompeiian boy becomes apprenticed to a physician as the volcano Vesuvius smoulders in the background.
  [1. Pompeii (Ancient city)—Fiction.   2. Apprentices—Fiction] I. Title.
PZ7.Y1954Lo 1984   [Fic]   84-47632
ISBN 0-06-026636-8
ISBN 0-06-026637-6 (lib. bdg.)

1

Only one thing marred the perfect blue of the sky, and that was the jaunty plume of smoke over the cone of Vesuvius. Very few of the people in Pompeii gave the volcano any notice, except to boast of it to strangers.

Neither Enecus Cano nor his good friend Salvius Valens paid attention to it; they were sitting on the embankment near the quay, watching the merchant ships unload. Both of them had other work to do but had slipped away for a few hours in the sun where they could talk without being disturbed by their families.

"Is your father still determined for you to go into

the business?" Enecus asked Salvius, shading his eyes from the glint of the sun.

"That's why he tells me," Salvius answered darkly, "that he doesn't mind me watching the ships. He wants me to have my own ship for a few years and later take over his job." He stretched out lazily, leaning against the embankment. "I wouldn't mind the ship, but I'd want to do something more than be a cloth merchant."

"Oh?" Enecus responded, his hazel eyes full of mischief. "Does that mean you want to be a pirate?"

"By Neptune, no!" Salvius protested, and then realized that Enecus had been teasing him. "Of course not," he went on, more mildly. "But can you think what it would be like to take a bireme and head out of the Portals of Hercules to the great ocean, and then go south into Africa...?"

"You can do that now. All you have to do is cross the Mediterranean to Carthago or to Hippo Regius," Enecus pointed out.

But Salvius scoffed at the idea. "Three to five days aboard! What's the use of that? Don't you want to see the men of Britannia, all painted blue?"

"Are you sure they aren't blue from the cold?" Enecus suggested. "Look at that ship!" he interrupted himself, pointing along the quay to where a trireme with strange devices painted on her sails was maneuvering toward the wharves. "What do you suppose that is?"

Salvius knew more about ships than Enecus, so he answered in an offhand way, "That's one of those marble ships from Ephesus. They're built to ride low in the water, or they couldn't carry all that stone. Probably got cargo for the Temple of Apollo." He rarely had the chance to be better informed than Enecus, and he could not help but make the most of his opportunity. "They say that the marble from Chios and Lesbos is better."

"Who says so?" Enecus asked, curious as always.

"I heard my brother say that the priests at the Temple of Venus wanted marble from Chios and could not get it." He thought for a moment, then said, "Britannia is north, isn't it?"

"Yes," Enecus answered, smiling slightly.

"I didn't *think* it was in Africa," Salvius muttered. "But they *do* paint themselves blue, for all that. The people of Africa are all black."

"And you're going to be all red if you stay in the sun much longer," warned Enecus.

"Then I'll match your hair," Salvius snapped. He decided to change the subject. "Has your father made plans for you yet?"

"He keeps saying that he ought to teach me how to run the thermopolium, but I don't want to spend the rest of my life selling wine and beer and sausages to anyone with half a denarius." He scowled. "I wish he'd buy me an apprenticeship."

"As what this week?" Salvius taunted, remembering how often Enecus changed his mind.

"Well, I did want to talk to one of the bestiarii from the amphitheater, but most animal trainers are born to it, not apprenticed, so that's out." With a sigh he turned away from the water and looked north where Vesuvius loomed. "I don't want to be apprenticed to Italicus and do nothing but make saddles and bridles and yokes for the rest of my days, though it's a good trade."

"I suppose my father might take you on somewhere," Salvius said. "We could work together."

Enecus shook his head. "Your father wouldn't do that. He can't afford it, even if he agreed. Your brothers have reason to want to work in the business, and you know that he can't prefer me to them." He tugged at the belt of his tunica. "At least all we have to wear are gold rings when we reach fourteen. Not like the equestrians and senators, with their togas."

Salvius laughed. "My father has two of them, for formal banquets, and all he ever does is get tangled up in them. A tunica or a dalmatica should be enough for any man."

"We aren't men yet," Enecus reminded him.

"Well, I'll be fourteen in two months, and you'll be fourteen in December. That's close enough." He thrust out his jaw. "You'd better know what you want to do by then. Your father will have to file his testament with the magistrates then, no matter what you decide."

Enecus did not answer for a little while, letting his mind drift as he watched the black smoke from the volcano spiral slowly into the summer sky. "I might want to become a shipwright, something that really matters, so I can see my handiwork."

"Why not be a physician, then? You can see your

handiwork on the streets every day, if your patients recover." He slapped his thigh and chuckled at his own humor. "A ship, that's a challenge, but people— now there's a real contest for you."

"It costs too much money," Enecus said quietly. "I've already asked, but the thermopolium doesn't bring in enough money for my father to afford such an apprenticeship."

This was the first time Salvius realized that his friend was seriously interested in medicine, and it startled him. "You already asked? You didn't say anything to me about it."

Enecus stared away from Salvius, his eyes troubled. "I didn't think it would be possible. I just thought I'd find out, in case . . . " He ran his hand through his hair; it was curly and the dark red color of Gallic bricks. His father's hair was more the shade of rust, but his sister's was bright red, with long wavy tresses that Enecus said looked like a fire in a hayrick.

"How much was it?" Salvius could not resist asking.

"A lot of money. More than we paid for Mnendos." If an education cost more than a slave, he knew that his family would not be able to afford it.

"But . . ." Salvius began, then stopped. "I suppose you haven't any rich relatives that might help out?"

"You know better," Enecus said morosely. "There's that uncle of my mother's, the dyer in Corinthus, but he has six children of his own to care for."

"Besides, he's Greek, isn't he?" Salvius said.

"My mother's Greek," Enecus reminded him sharply.

Salvius shook his head. "Not the same thing. She is married to a Roman citizen, isn't she, even if your father's people came from Gallia. Ledosus, wasn't it? Where they make that pottery?"

"That's right. My grandfather was born there," Enecus said.

"Well, my grandfather was born here, and his grandfather was, and—" He fell silent, recognizing the boastful sound in his own voice that so irritated him in his father.

"We're all Romans," Enecus said, getting to his feet. "They'll need me at the thermopolium. Business gets pretty brisk by late afternoon. That's when we sell the most sausages, especially those long plump ones wrapped in bread."

"I like those," Salvius said, grinning. "Put two on the grill for me, will you?"

Enecus made a face. "All right. But if you had to cook as many of them as I have, you'd hate the sight of them." He dusted off the back of his tunica and tightened his belt. "Come on."

"Oh, all right," Salvius said, pretending to grumble as he got to his feet. "I suppose I have to come with you if I want those sausages."

"You idiot," Enecus said, feinting to punch his friend in the arm. Before Salvius could retaliate, Enecus had sprinted away toward the Porta Marina, laughing as Salvius hurried after him.

The streets were crowded, but the boys made good time, dashing past the Temple of Venus, then running

6

toward the Forum Civilis, dodging pedestrians and chair carriers expertly.

There were two tribunes carrying on a debate in the Forum, and here Enecus and Salvius had to push their way through the crowd that had stopped to listen.

"Politicians!" Salvius scoffed when they had got through the crush. "All they ever do is talk!"

"That Urbanis Agrippus Quintus is a fool," Enecus declared, repeating what his father had said.

"Don't be silly," Salvius protested. "He's had years more experience than Flavius Constantinus Draco."

The two boys were still arguing when they came to the thermopolium with the bright red rooster painted on the awning.

The Gallus Rubeus was a popular place, and there were half a dozen people standing at the street-side counter waiting for their orders to be filled. Someone always made the same pun about the name of the place, changing the words slightly to mean, instead of the Red Cockerel, the Red-Haired Gaul. Enecus' father did not mind these jokes, accepting them with unfailing good humor, knowing that the customers would remember his place and return.

This afternoon, Enecus' mother was serving the sausages while his father poured out the wine and beer from large kegs set into holes in the counter. When he saw his son approaching, Amalius Cano raised his hand and waved. "There you are!"

Enecus waved back. "I've been ... running errands."

"At the harbor, no doubt," Amalius said kindly. "Never mind that now. Wash up and give your mother a hand."

"Should I come back later?" Salvius asked, seeing how busy the thermopolium was.

"No. I'll fix some sausages for you," Enecus promised. He slipped between two customers and ducked under the counter.

"We need more of the skewers from the back," his mother said as she caught sight of him. "I'll put the sausages on for Salvius." She gave Enecus a quick wink, then went back to turning the sausages that simmered on the grill.

The small room was hot and smelled redolently of meat and spices, but Enecus scarcely noticed as he ducked through the curtained doorway into the rear of the food shop. He sighed as he washed his hands, and he sighed again as he tied a mantile around his waist to protect his tunica from the spattering grease. He found the skewers and took them to his mother, resigned to spending the evening at the grill.

The oil lamps gave the family kitchen a cheery glow, but the four family members seated at the square table in the center of the room were somber.

"We have to make a decision, Enecus, you know that. We must file something before too long or the magistrates might decide on their own. That might not be to anyone's liking." Amalius leaned his thick arms on the table as he stared at his son. "We have Pyralis to think of, as well."

"I don't mind sharing the thermopolium with Enecus," his sister said. "I'd like to have him here."

"Unfortunately, that's an arrangement the magistrates wouldn't approve of," Amalius declared. "Each of you must be provided for, and if you shared the business, it would have to be sacrificed if one of you married. So only one of you can inherit it, and the other must be apprenticed. We don't have anyone in the family to apprentice Pyralis to, unless we send her to your mother's people in Greece. It must be you, Enecus, who is the apprentice." They all knew this, but as Amalius repeated it, the burden of it struck them anew. "I don't know what to do if you will not choose a profession."

"Well," Enecus said reluctantly, "I have said it would not be bad to make boats. I'd like that better than saddlery."

"But it is not what you want most, is it?" his mother asked.

"No," Enecus admitted. "But we can't afford what I want."

Amalius brought his head up; he had been staring down into his earthenware cup. "What *do* you want, son?"

"To be a physician," Enecus said sadly. "And I have already discovered what the cost of such an apprenticeship is. I do not know if there is enough money in all the family to purchase it."

"A physician?" Rhea said, looking at her son thoughtfully. "How long have you wanted that?"

9

"Don't make it worse, love," Amalius cautioned her, but Enecus answered.

"For two, three years. Ever since I watched the men being treated who were brought off that battered ship. I saw what the physicians did, and I thought I would like to do that, too. They closed wounds and ended the pain and . . . many of the sailors lived who would otherwise have died." Saying it aloud made him feel foolish, and he blushed bright as his hair. "I don't mean that lightly."

"Of course not," Rhea soothed him.

"Do you *really* want to do that?" Pyralis asked, amazed. "I don't think I could stand it, all those broken bones and sick people. Ugh!"

"But I could make them better," Enecus said patiently. "I know I could, if I had someone to teach me how. I don't think anything would be better than doing that."

Amalius nodded and exchanged a regretful look with his wife.

Pyralis went on as if no one else had spoken. "I'd rather have people around me who are merry and joking, who smile when I pour them wine and grill up sausages."

"You see?" Enecus said. "This is the place for you, and your life. You are happy here. You like to work here, and at the end of the day you are proud of what you've done, of the food you have served and sold. It just bores me."

"Bores you?" Pyralis shrieked. "How can something

10

as exciting as the thermopolium bore you? All those people, all their conversations, all that hustle and bustle." Her eyes sparkled. "I think this must be one of the most exciting kinds of work in the world. Not like taking care of open wounds."

Enecus shrugged. "It doesn't matter. We can't afford it, anyway."

Amalius started to speak, but Rhea interrupted him before his first word was out. "There may be a way. Not all physicians take care only of the rich. There are some who look after us, and they are not as demanding. It may be that they look for apprentices as well."

"They have sons to think of," Amalius muttered.

"Possibly," Rhea conceded but continued cheerfully. "But it may be that we can find one. We still have four months before we must present our testament to the magistrates. In that time, who knows what we can learn? Half of Pompeii must come under our awning in the course of a year. Surely someone will have a suggestion."

"You don't want to get his hopes up, love," Amalius warned her.

"But I don't want him to abandon them, either," she said. "In four months, if we have not found a physician who will take you on as an apprentice at a price we can afford, then we will speak to Gaius the boatwright; he always needs apprentices." She looked over her shoulder toward the front room of their apartment, where the household slave was lighting the lamps. "Mnendos!"

11

"Yes?" he called back gruffly.

"When you take your leisure with the other slaves, will you ask around, to discover who the ordinary physicians are, and what kind of reputations they have?" She grinned at Enecus, repeating an old saying: "Slaves know everything."

Enecus only sighed.

"Don't be downhearted, Enecus," Pyralis said. "Mnendos can find out anything. He found out who stole the spices from the kitchen that time." She patted her brother's arm. "I'll listen more closely to what I hear in the thermopolium. I'll ask questions. It will work out; you'll see."

"I hope so," Enecus said with a wan, unhopeful smile.

II

For two weeks Enecus and his family were disappointed by what they found; then on a sultry afternoon when business had slowed for an hour or so, Hercules Impatus lumbered under the awning and bawled out a friendly greeting to Amalius, who was using the slack time to pile up more sausages by the grill.

"How long has it been?" Amalius roared out, a huge smile spreading over his square features. "You're looking fit!"

Hercules had been with the Cat's Paw Legion for fifteen years and now worked as a trainer of charioteers. He was a squat, massive man with tree-trunk legs and enormous shoulders. "I'd better be," he answered. "Those youngsters I'm teaching are harder to work with than green recruits." He took the cup offered him and drank deeply before holding out a silver coin.

"Never mind that," Amalius said, waving the money away. "Tell me how it's been going. What brings you all the way from Acerrae to Pompeii? This isn't a racing day."

"Oh, one of my new ones went and dislocated his shoulder overtaxing the horses on a practice run. Terrible thing. We did what we could for him, but the swelling got out of hand." He finished his wine and accepted a refill. "I can't tell you what it's been like since old Gobius the horse handler bought his freedom. We're working three times as hard with half the results."

"Wait a moment," Amalius said, his thoughts changing swiftly. "You brought your charioteer into the city? Why not—"

Hercules laughed. "I'm not about to trust one of these boys to a country physician. I'm not such a fool. Give me a man who's been with the Legions—now, *there's* a physician you can trust, not like the snobs at the main house, or the Greeks with their lotions and pomanders."

"But . . ." Amalius tried to contain his enthusiasm. "A Legion physician, here in Pompeii? I don't know about such a man." Not that he had not asked, he reflected with bitter amusement as he waited for Hercules to finish his wine and answer the question.

"He's not the sort who goes looking for business.

14

Not his style. That's one of the reasons he left the Cat's Paw—too much to do, and he was starting to get old." Hercules pulled up one of the three stools by the counter and hitched himself onto it.

"And he probably wanted to settle his family," Amalius suggested, hoping he might learn something more.

"Too late for that. His wife died of the fever in Gaza, years ago, before they had children." He pointed to the long sausages that were stacked by the grill. "Cook me up a couple of those, will you? And give them to me wrapped in bread."

"Glad to," Amalius said, putting the sausages onto the grill. "An old man, this physician?"

"About forty, forty-five. Quick mind, sharp tongue. He knows his work, no question about it." He paused. "Why are you so interested in him? Got illness in the family?"

"Oh, nothing like that," Amalius said. "But you know how it is—every now and then someone gets burned, or there's a scuffle in the street. I always like to have a name so I can send for help that won't be more expensive than it's worth."

Hercules nodded. "Well, you won't find Locadio Priscus demanding a pouchful of gold coins every time he looks in your ears."

"Locadio Priscus?" Amalius repeated the name. "Where is he?"

"Oh, over by the Porta Capua, on the Via Palma. Not a fancy place, but he has work enough in his infirmary." He took the first bread-wrapped sausage.

15

"Isn't old Sestus Loquax still taking care of your family? He's a good physician."

Amalius sighed. "Not for this." In a sudden burst of candor, he explained his predicament to his friend, while Hercules listened and ate.

"Well, I don't know how to advise you," Hercules said when he had heard Amalius out. "All fathers have such choices to make, but in a case like this, where a good sum of money is involved . . ." He ate the last of his sausage. "You know what the world is like."

"None better," Amalius said wearily.

"Still, it can't hurt to talk to the man, can it? He hasn't got sons, and if there are nephews, I never heard of one. It can't hurt to talk to the man."

"I suppose not," Amalius said, brightening a little. "On the Via Palma, you say?"

"Near the Porta Capua. He's got a place of his own across from a block of red-fronted insulae." Hercules stood up. "I hope it turns out well for your boy. He's a good fellow, isn't he?"

"That he is," Amalius agreed. "I want to do my best for him."

"What good father does not?" He once more offered coins, and again Amalius refused them.

"If my son gets an apprenticeship from this, it is the best trade I've ever had on wine and sausage."

Hercules did not argue; he smiled and waved. "Tell your wife and family I send my greetings to them." With that, he strolled away whistling.

16

Amalius took a deep breath, then called for Mnendos.

The two slaves looked each other over carefully.

"What do you wish of me?" Vibian asked Mnendos in his most polite manner.

"I carry a message from my master to your master." Mnendos folded his arms over his chest and waited.

"If it is a matter of illness—" Vibian began.

"It is not," Mnendos cut in. "I have said it is a message."

Vibian was about to turn Mnendos away from the door when he heard someone in the room behind him.

"What is it, Vibian?" Locadio asked, sounding as if he were half asleep.

"A slave with a message, master," Vibian answered. "He says it is not about illness."

"A pleasant change," Locadio observed, coming toward the door. He was dressed in a worn tunica and wore old military sandals laced up his legs. "Who is your master, slave, and what does he want of me?"

Mnendos cleared his throat. "My master is Amalius Cano, owner of the Gallus Rubeus, a thermopolium on the Via Porta Vesuvius."

"I'm not one to go out for sausage. Vibian does my cooking for me," Locadio said, preparing to turn away.

"It's not that," Mnendos said quickly. "My master has a son, thirteen, who wants to become a physician." He had said it too fast; proper form required that he

17

present this information in an ordered way, and he was ashamed that he had not.

Locadio stood still, looking closely at Mnendos. "A boy out of a thermopolium is scarcely in a position to be an apprentice physician."

"That is what he fears, but he . . . it is what he wishes most to do, and his father must apprentice him before December. If you are not willing to discuss the matter, then we must look elsewhere." Mnendos was very disappointed.

"Why not send him to Pisae or Ancona?" He shook his head. "It might be best if he set his sights on other work."

"He will, if it is not possible to apprentice him to a physician," Mnendos said, his face turning sad. "I will tell my master that you—"

Locadio interrupted him. "You will tell your master that you have given me the message he sent and that I have said I will think about it and will send him word shortly." He glanced at Vibian, who clearly disapproved of everything he had heard. "It is not good conduct to refuse out of hand, Vibian. You have reminded me of that on many occasions in the past."

Vibian made an exasperated noise. "Master, it is not right to raise hope where none can be fulfilled." He was older than his owner by fifteen years and had the habit of speaking to Locadio as if to a half-grown boy. "Think what your answer might imply."

"It implies only that I will think it over," Locadio said patiently. "There is nothing wrong in that." He looked

18

at Mnendos. "Please give your master my message. Do not elaborate it, and do not change it. He will have my answer soon." Saying that, he turned around and wandered back into the cool darkness of his reception room.

Vibian looked toward Mnendos but not at him. "You heard my master. You will carry out his instructions."

"High-nosed fellow, aren't you?" Mnendos asked with a short laugh. "Your master is less haughty than you." Pleased with this parting shot, he turned on his heel and strode away toward the Via Oraculi.

Two days later, Locadio dressed in an old dalmatica, belting it with a leather strap, and put on his Greek-style sandals, then set out for the Gallus Rubeus. He could feel Vibian's outrage as he went, for the old slave hated to see his master dress in a manner not appropriate for a person of his station and rank.

Amalius was in the back chopping meat, and it was Rhea who greeted Locadio as he sat down, ordering the spicy round sausages, on skewers, and wine.

As she filled his cup, she said, "I believe I have not seen you before, good stranger."

"You have not," Locadio said in a tone that discouraged more conversation. He drank slowly and watched the sausages cooking.

Rhea shrugged and went back to her work, pausing occasionally to call to friends who passed in the street. Locadio watched all this, listening to everything that went on.

In a little while, Pyralis came through the curtain from the back. "The new sausages are almost finished. I'm going over to Antonius' bakery for more bread. Do you need anything else?"

Rhea turned to her daughter. "Tell Antonius that we will want more of those buns filled with dates. Ask for two dozen and settle for sixteen if you must."

Pyralis grinned, tossing her head. "I will get two dozen, wait and see."

"No doubt," Rhea said, adding to Locadio, "Daughters!" as Pyralis left the thermopolium.

"Seems bright enough," Locadio responded.

"Both our children have ability," Rhea said, pausing thoughtfully while she turned the sausages. "We're fortunate."

"Um." Locadio took another small sip of wine; he had no desire to fuddle his senses while he waited to get a look at this son of theirs.

Rhea poked a skewer through the round sausages and handed it to Locadio, then turned to serve wine to three fellows who came ambling up to the street-side counter.

Then there was a commotion, and two half-grown young men ducked under the counter and rushed toward the grill.

"Enecus!" Rhea called out.

He turned when he heard his name. "Sorry, Mother. It took longer than usual to get Juvus to come down in his price. He'll deliver the meat tomorrow morning, before the gates open." He tried to stop his friend from reaching toward the grill.

"Ow!" Salvius wailed as his fingers blistered in the sudden spattering of grease.

Enecus grabbed Salvius' hand. "Don't put more grease on it; it will only make it worse if you do," he said firmly.

From his place on the stool, Locadio raised his brows in surprise. He listened more closely.

"But it hurts!" Salvius protested, trying to pull his hand free from Enecus' grip.

"Naturally, since you put it near metal over hot coals," Enecus pointed out. "You have to expect—"

"Give me back my hand!" Salvius yelled as Enecus tugged him into the back of the thermopolium.

"I have some paste made with plantain and raspberry and willow bark," Enecus said steadily. "That will help."

"By Mars and Venus!" Salvius swore.

"If a little burn makes you scream like this, what happens to you in battle? What would the Legions think of you?" Enecus teased as the curtain closed behind them.

"Boys." Rhea sighed, glancing at Locadio. "You have children of your own?"

"No."

Rhea nodded, not at all put off by his bad manners.

Locadio was busy listening to what was happening behind the curtain.

"Hold still," Enecus told his friend.

"Oh, all right," Salvius replied in a sulky voice. "That stuff looks terrible."

"It's not so bad. It'll take the sting out." There was silence for a moment, and then Enecus went on. "There. I'll wrap it up, and in a little while it should be much better. We're always getting little burns around here. That's how I know about the paste."

"Well . . ." Salvius said uncertainly.

"Leave it alone. I'll wrap it." Again there was silence, and then Amalius cut in.

"What's going on here, you two?"

"Oh, Salvius got burned, and I was taking care of him" came Enecus' very casual answer. "See? I just finished wrapping it up. I did it really well, didn't I?"

"Yes," Amalius answered heavily. "Listen, Enecus, don't spend too much time on this. It might turn out that we cannot obtain that apprenticeship for you, and I do not want you to be cast down if it turns out that way."

There was a pause. "If Enecus joins the Legions, he could learn to be a physician," Salvius said.

"My son does not need to join the Legions," Amalius declared. "We are not fighting men in this family—we are peaceful folk, who tend to our business and stay away from battle."

"I'd want to be in the Legions," Salvius insisted. "I would want to go as far as the Empire extends, and then go beyond that. There's not enough adventure here."

"Tell me that after you have ridden out a storm at sea," Enecus teased him. "Or burned your whole hand. I did that once. I felt sick from it."

"That's not the same thing as an adventure," Salvius protested. "Facing a host of enemies in golden armor with battle hammers and archers, *that's* an adventure. If all I ever do is buy cloth, what does it matter where the merchant lives, or what color the skin of the weaver is? It's still only so much cloth."

"There are many who would not agree. Some might like their adventure with a little less battle," Enecus suggested.

Salvius laughed. "Where is the thrill without the risk?"

"Well, I didn't say I did not want risk, I just don't want to . . ." He lifted the curtain and started out toward the grill again.

"But there's no other way," Salvius explained, following him, but avoiding the grill. Two fingers of his left hand were carefully but inexpertly bandaged.

"I did not say there was. I only said that I wish there were." He reached for one of the skewers and caught a sausage on the pointed end. He handed this to Salvius. "Go on. You deserve it."

Salvius accepted the sausage in silence. Locadio got up, leaving behind two copper coins and a silver piece.

III

A procession was on its way to the Temple of Apollo, winding through the streets of Pompeii and causing delays to one-man chariots, sedan chairs and pedestrians alike. Musicians and priests led the parade, singing the praises of their god while the people lining the streets cheered or grumbled at the spectacle. A brisk breeze from the sea kept the afternoon from being too hot, though August often sweltered.

"It won't be more than an hour," Pyralis argued, poking her brother in the ribs. "We have to be ready. That one vat is only half filled with wine."

"We don't want it to go sour," Enecus reminded

her. "You know what Mother said the last time that happened."

Pyralis put her hands on her hips. She was lanky and leggy but showed promise for turning into one of those slender, lithe girls who were always compared to wood nymphs. "But if there are lots of cups to fill, it won't have time to go sour."

"I think we ought to wait," Enecus insisted. He had to shout to be heard over the noise of the procession, even though it was a block away.

"You don't want to work!" Pyralis told him. "You're grumpy because you think you'll have to be a ship-wright instead of a physician."

This was very nearly the truth, but Enecus denied it. "I just don't want our parents getting angry with us for ruining the wine."

"We should have more to offer than wine and beer," Pyralis said, suddenly changing the subject. "When this is my thermopolium, I want to change it so that it isn't just for a quick bite to eat and a cup of wine. I want it to be more like the place that Petros has, on the Via Legati, with tables and a bigger menu."

"You want to change this to a . . . a tratorium? This place?" Enecus blinked in surprise. "Do you know how much work there is in a place like that? It isn't enough to have the grill, you know; you must also have ovens and . . . all the rest of it. You will have to arrange for meats and vegetables and fruits every day, and you'll need at least one more slave to serve the customers."

Pyralis raised her chin. "I know all that. It doesn't bother me."

"But—" Enecus broke off. "Well, if there's a way you can do it, then I hope you can, Pyralis."

Her expression softened a little. "And I hope a physician takes you as apprentice." She decided to take advantage of his good humor. "And I hope you will bring the wine in and fill the vat before the procession is finished."

Enecus watched her flounce out of range, laughing when she lifted the curtain between the front and the back of the thermopolium. "You're pushing your luck, girl."

"I know," she called happily.

Business had been so brisk that it was quite dark by the time Amalius and Rhea closed up the front of the thermopolium and climbed the stairs to their apartment above it.

"A profitable day," Rhea said as she counted the coins in the leather pouch that hung from her belt. "Processions bring out people's thirst."

Amalius grunted his agreement. He had been calling out greetings and food orders for so long that his voice was hoarse from it. They reached their apartment and went in.

Mnendos waited for them, an excited expression on his face. "There was a message, master," he said, almost hopping up and down with delight. "The slave of the physician Locadio Priscus came today and said that his master would call tomorrow evening to discover what terms of apprenticeship are acceptable to you, and to see if an agreement can be reached."

Amalius looked up, his hazel eyes opening wide. "What did you say?"

"Have you told Enecus yet?" Rhea asked, as amazed as her husband.

"Enecus knows nothing," Mnendos assured them. "That way, if it comes to nothing, he will not be as upset. I have taken it upon myself to say that you will speak to the man as soon as he arrives."

Amalius slapped his hand to his forehead. "I'm having two casks of wine delivered tomorrow."

"I will manage that," Rhea said in her practical way. "I will tend to it while you speak to this physician. And stop worrying, my husband. If you don't, I promise I will scorch your cheese in the morning."

That made Amalius smile. "Well, for all we know, he is going to make impossible terms. Then the negotiations will be swift, if a little disappointing. These physicians are a strange lot."

"Do not make up his mind for him," Rhea warned her husband. "You will not be able to learn anything until the man comes here, so do not wrack your mind with idle speculation. You will hear soon enough." She put her arm around his waist. "If it works out well, I will burn incense to Isis every night from now until the dead of winter."

"Well, if you think it would help . . . I can offer prayers to Apollo." He hugged her back. "That boy is capable and bright. But a physician's life is hard, and it may be that he would prefer a less arduous trade."

"Amalius, if you don't stop, I promise you I will batter your head," Rhea said, laughing with vexation. "You can be the most *impossible* man."

Amalius kissed her forehead. "I will try to be patient," he said, and Rhea was forced to be content with that.

Locadio entered the thermopolium as the sun was setting. This time he was more correctly attired for a man of his profession; he wore a blue-colored wide-skirted garment called a synthesis with a single stripe running down its front and back. His belt was brass-studded leather, and he had stout soldier's shoes on his feet. At Vibian's insistence, he carried his physician's staff.

Amalius had been growing more nervous about the visit, and by midafternoon he had found it almost impossible to keep up with the ordinary demands of his work. The relief he felt at the sight of the physician made him dizzy. "Good evening to you," he said, surprised at how gruff he sounded.

"And to you," Locadio answered. "I am Locadio Priscus."

"I am Amalius Cano," he replied, reaching out to take the physician's wrist in his hand.

"I understand that you are willing to enter into an apprenticeship contract on behalf of your son." He knew that he was being more stuffy than usual, but he felt awkward in this situation and did not know how to conduct himself.

"Yes, yes. Come in, Priscus. Let me take you upstairs, to our private quarters. We may be more comfortable there." Amalius hurried to put the thermopolium in order, then called to his daughter. "You finish closing up, Pyralis. And then go help your mother in the storeroom."

Pyralis could not resist poking her head through the curtain to get a glimpse of their visitor. She was not impressed with what she saw, but she smiled as she often smiled at customers and told her father that she was glad to help him.

"Good girl, Pyralis," Amalius said, needing to say something as he led his guest to the stairs and up them to the reception room, where Mnendos was lighting the wicks of the oil lamps. "Both the children are worthwhile, industrious."

"That must be a great joy to you," Locadio responded stiffly. "A family is always fortunate in virtuous children."

"And the gods smile when they grant such," Amalius said, standing aside to permit Locadio to choose a chair.

When he was seated and Amalius had drawn up one of the padded benches, Locadio decided he might as well get it all over with. "I have not taken on an apprentice before. I am not a physician who has such a practice that I thought it was necessary. But I am getting older, and I know that there are tasks I will not always be able to perform. Rather than jeopardize my patients, I have decided to consider your offer."

Amalius nodded. "We are not rich. I make reasonable money for a man in my line of work, but our means are limited."

"As are mine. If you want your son to be at the right hand of the Emperor, then you must look elsewhere for his training." He cleared his throat. "I was with the Cat's Paw, and I have many regular patients. I earn an adequate amount, but I do not live in luxury. I practice my craft as best as I know how."

"What man can do more?" Amalius observed. "I can think of no one who can desire more than that."

Locadio decided he would not debate the matter; he pressed on. "You must not hope that your son will excel at this profession, even if he does have an aptitude for it, in less than five years. That would mean that we must make provision for a review of his development at regular intervals as long as the contract is in force. It is obvious to me that because of the circumstances, I cannot promise your son employment when his training is completed, because we do not yet know that his training will be completed, or what level of skill he will obtain."

"That is reasonable," Amalius allowed, his worry increasing.

"And until the boy has shown skill, I will not want him living under my roof. If we agree on terms, one of them must be that he live with you for the first year of the apprenticeship, until I have had time to assess his temperament." He paused. "An adjustment of the fees paid would be in order for that year, of course."

Amalius nodded. "I am certain we can make such a provision."

They turned as Mnendos came back into the front room with a tray. Two cups of wine—Amalius knew from the color of the jug beside them that it was the best they had to offer—and a dish of raisin buns were set on it. "Your wife told me to bring this," Mnendos announced to Amalius, trying not to stare at Locadio.

"Thank her for me," Locadio said before Amalius could speak. "It is a generous thing to offer such hospitality."

"I will tell her," Mnendos said, grinning, as he left the room.

Amalius was used to serving food, and quite automatically held out the larger cup to Locadio, spilling a drop in libation to the gods before he drank. "She is a good woman, my wife."

Locadio was pleasantly surprised at the quality of the wine, and relaxed enough to say so.

"My daughter is the one who selects the wines now. She's only twelve, but she knows more than the rest of us put together, and that includes Mnendos. That is why I am especially anxious to leave the thermopolium to her, since it is what she wishes most to do. Enecus is not too interested in this occupation and has told me that more than anything he wishes to be a physician." He drank more of the wine, hoping that his candor had not offended Locadio.

31

"Desire is not the same as experience," Locadio said thoughtfully. "But it may be that he has the ability. We will discover that soon enough."

Amalius turned toward his guest. "Then you will take him? Though we cannot offer much money?"

Locadio chuckled. "I will need five silver denarii at the start of each month, and—"

"Five? Is that all?" Amalius was startled at the low figure.

"I will also expect dining privileges here for me, for your son, and for my infirmary slave. He's something of an upstart, who hasn't learned the difference between men and animals yet. His name is Granius. I will not expect you to feed my majordomo. In addition, at the first of each year the contract is in force, I will require the payment of thirty aurei."

"Thirty?" Amalius exclaimed. "I haven't twenty of them to spare at the end of a year. This is a business that deals in silver, not gold."

"Yes." Locadio nodded. "I am willing to negotiate on that, for I have need of herbs and spices for medications, and if you are willing to supply them to me—for you can purchase them at a lowered rate for your cooking—then some of that figure may be reduced."

"It will have to be, if we are to enter a contract," Amalius said heavily. He poured more wine into Locadio's cup, then helped himself. "Thirty aurei. I am fortunate to see one aureus a month. Thirty in a year is beyond me."

Locadio rubbed his forehead with his free hand. "It may be that we will find another way."

"We must, if my son is to be your apprentice." Amalius thought. "We will get the herbs and spices for you. That I am willing to do. I am also willing to provide any other supplies that you may need that I am in a position to purchase at a reduced rate. There must be other things you need—plates, jars, knives—that will take the place of so much gold."

"It is possible," Locadio allowed. "Let us say that we will fix the aurei to be paid when the first year is over. For the time being, I will ask the customary fifteen, with the balance to be had in supplies." He drank, then put the cup down. "I'm not used to haggling this way, Cano. I would prefer to leave this to the advocates in the magistrates' offices to decide it, but they will take forever, and in the end, it will only add to the cost of the contract. Let us leave this for the time being and decide on how long it will take before you and I will be satisfied that the boy is capable or incapable of this work."

Amalius was not as pleased with the notion as Locadio was. "I dislike leaving such large amounts unsettled."

Locadio leaned back in the chair. "If your son increases my income, then half of what he earns will count toward the thirty aurei, as well as any supplies you obtain for me. Unless the boy is a dunce, you should have nothing to worry about." He reached for

33

one of the buns, breaking it open in the traditional manner. "Well?"

"I will consider it," he said, at last taking one of the buns himself. "But I would be displeased if you make the contract for less than three years before you refuse my son further instruction."

"Three years is reasonable, with two more should he prove apt. In those years, your payments would be reduced to the denarii and nothing more. That way I will not have spent my time for nothing and you will not be tempted to withdraw your son before he has had sufficient chance to prove himself." He ate half the bun, glad that this meeting was almost over.

"I will agree to that," Amalius said quickly.

"If the boy falls ill or in some way is rendered unable to continue his apprenticeship, I will accept the usual termination fee." He paused. "If I cannot continue his instruction, I will arrange for another physician to see him through his apprenticeship. Is that satisfactory?"

Amalius was far more pleased than he admitted, even to himself. He had been afraid that the training would be too costly and the terms of the apprenticeship too limiting for any reasonable man to accept them. Now he was confident that Enecus would have the opportunity he longed for. "Yes, I believe that is satisfactory."

"Then have the magistrates examine the contract within the month and we will commence at once." He started to get up, then looked at Enecus' father. "Do you wish to introduce me to your son now, or would

34

you prefer to wait until the contract is signed?"

"It is more customary to wait," Amalius said slowly, then shook his head, clapping his hands loudly. "Mnendos! Is Enecus about?"

The slave came back into the room so quickly that both Amalius and Locadio were certain he had been listening to their conversation. "He is not here, master. He has gone to eat with Salvius. Your wife thought it might be best."

Amalius agreed at once. "Probably." He made a gesture of dismissal and gave his attention once more to Locadio. "We will do it the more traditional way."

"Whatever is satisfactory," Locadio said, starting to get to his feet. "Are you going to inform the boy of this meeting?"

"Yes; when he returns home," Amalius said, rising with his guest.

"Excellent. Then I will wait for word from you that the contract is prepared. As soon as you are ready, I will send you a voucher for the magistrates." He almost forgot his staff, but reached for it before he left the room.

Locadio wanted to admit that he had already observed Enecus, which would have been embarrassing for both men, and so he said nothing but the socially proper things before leaving Amalius to carry the news to the rest of the family.

"So," Enecus explained excitedly to Salvius the next day, "I will live with my family for the first year, then

35

go to the house of this physician Locadio Priscus for another two years, and if I do well, then I will study with him for two more years."

Salvius pretended to punch Enecus in the shoulder. "What's so special about that? Most apprenticeships are for five years."

"But this is with a *physician*," Enecus said, as if the word were foreign to his friend.

"And I will spend five years learning to evaluate cloth. At the end of that time, we will both have to make our way in the world, no matter what those five years bring. If you discover you have made an error in judgment, what then?" They had just come through the market-place, and each of them had bought something—Salvius had purchased a bath kit on a bronze ring, with an oil jar and scrapers; Enecus, a set of old-fashioned wax tablets and a stylus so that he could take notes during his instruction.

"Then I will have to find other work without the aid of my father. As will you, if you do not want to buy cloth." He tugged Salvius to the side of the road so that a large, enclosed sedan chair with four bearers could get past them.

"Old cow!" Salvius yelled after the sedan chair. Then he turned to Enecus. "If I don't stay with the business, then I will join the Legions and go fight in Germania or Gallia or Armenia."

"But we are at peace in most of those places," Enecus pointed out.

Salvius pouted. "It won't last. And even if it does, it

would be more exciting than being a mercer. That's enough for me."

"If you expand the business, you will go to Gallia and Germania and Armenia and all the rest of those places, so why join the Legions?"

"It would be . . . better," Salvius insisted.

"Or it could be worse, if you were to be hurt. You're my friend, Salvius. I would not want you to be wounded, or worse." He ran a few paces to get away from another one of Salvius' wild punches. "Come on. I'll have Pyralis make some of those long sausages for us."

"All right," Salvius said, letting their argument drop. "I don't think it's the same, being in the Legions or being a cloth merchant, do you? Mercers lead such quiet lives. If that's what I end up doing, I'll probably never see battle, will I?"

"Probably not," Enecus conceded, walking more quickly along the crowded street. "But you won't find out one way or the other until you try, and trading cloth is more pleasant."

"It's boring!" Salvius shouted.

"How do you know?" Enecus called back, certain that Salvius had no answer to his question.

IV

Locadio's infirmary was divided into three sections: The first chamber, which opened onto a passageway leading to the street, was lined with low benches and was where his patients and those accompanying them waited. The second room, just beyond this, was considerably larger, lit by several windows high in the white-washed walls. It was in this room that the greatest part of Locadio's treatments was provided. There was a third room beyond this, smaller than the second and more austere. It was in this room that Locadio isolated patients in need of surgery or the cauterizing of wounds.

"To start with," Locadio told Enecus the first day

he came to the infirmary, "you will take all the instruments and you will boil them, in this kettle here, with these herbs. You are to do this every time the instruments are used, both before and after, no exceptions."

"Very well," Enecus said, trying to appear as calm and prepared as possible. "When do you treat your patients?"

"When they come to me," Locadio answered. "They are the ones with the ills, not I. There are three that I know of who are coming in the afternoon, but who can tell if there will be others." He looked around the room. "The floors are to be washed every day, and if there is blood spilled, it is to be cleaned up immediately. You won't be faint at the sight of blood, I hope?"

"I don't think so. I've watched the Great Games," Enecus said, his confidence slightly shaken.

"It's not the same thing, boy," Locadio said grimly. "This is not the same as watching some gladiator on the sands get hacked by an opponent. You do not see those wounds. Here you must examine the hurts, and some are not pleasant. It is important that you remain calm, no matter what you see, for those who come here for help are frightened enough without seeing fear in your face or hearing it in your voice." He gave Enecus a thoughtful look. "I wonder if you can manage this."

"It is what I want to do," Enecus said, suddenly worried that Locadio might change his mind. "I am not afraid."

"Then you should be. What we do is difficult work,

and there is a high price to pay for errors. I do not want to have to remind you of that too often, boy. Now, start with the floors."

"All right," Enecus said, but without enthusiasm.

"What's the matter?" Locadio asked, hearing the hesitation in his tone.

"Oh . . . I guess I thought that there would be more to do," Enecus said, not quite truthfully.

Locadio understood at once. "You mean that you thought you would begin by saving lives the first thing you did. How were you planning to do that? By sorcery? You have not learned the beginning yet, and you wish to be at the end." He patted Enecus on the shoulder. "When you started to walk, you tottered as all children do, and it was a while before you could run. This is no different. At the moment, you can do little more than crawl, and it will take time before you are ready to jump hurdles." He almost smiled. "The floors. And do not expect my infirmary slave to do this; he has his hands full with taking care of those who come here. I rely on him to learn what he can of the patient and to make a first assessment of how serious the problem is." He started to walk away, then looked back at Enecus. "When the afternoon is over, we will go into the garden and I will answer your questions. Will that suit you, my eager young friend?"

"Yes," Enecus said, doing his best to keep from feeling disappointed. He did as he was told, gathering up the instruments and putting them to boil in the kettle with the astringent herbs added to the water. The brazier made the third room even hotter than the August sun, but he was determined to show how willing he was to accept all the conditions imposed on him.

At the end of the second week of his apprenticeship, Enecus saw his first real emergency, and all the precautions that Locadio had emphasized finally made sense to him.

He was just finishing grinding spices and herbs with mortar and pestle when he heard a sudden commotion in the outer room. At first he paid little heed to it, for he had come to realize that there were often such disruptions in a physician's day, most often requiring little more than a few words of reassurance and a salve to remedy. This was not the same. There were two or three voices, all raised in anger or excitement. Enecus listened, certain that the commotion would quiet down as soon as Locadio had had a chance to evaluate the situation.

But this did not happen. Enecus heard Locadio give a number of terse orders, and then, to his amazement, he heard his name called.

"I need my tools!" Locadio shouted. "Especially the ones for bleeding!"

Enecus hesitated, then reached for a clean section of cloth to carry the tools in, as he had been taught to do. He felt a touch of pride that Locadio should ask him to assist and was about to remark on it when he came through the door into the reception room and found a scene more suited to a battlefield than an infirmary.

Three men had been brought to Locadio, each of them badly injured, all of them bleeding. One of the men had been struck in the face by a chain, and his face was half raw. He held a hand to his nose, moaning, while blood leaked through his fingers.

The second man was badly bruised and there was a long scrape down the side of his leg that was already swollen and discolored. He was leaning on another man, who was unharmed but who clearly was more upset than the injured man he helped to support.

There was another badly hurt man, though at first Enecus could not see the reason for his pasty color and trembling hands. Then he took a more careful look and saw with a shock that the man's left shoulder was dislocated.

"They're workmen," Locadio said as he strove to staunch the bleeding on the first man. "Their scaffolding fell. They say that two men were killed."

Suddenly it was difficult for Enecus to swallow. "I..." he began, then faltered.

"My tools!" Locadio snapped. "Quickly!"

"I... it's..." Enecus gazed in horror at the man with the bleeding face. He had seen broken noses before, from street fights that erupted during festival seasons, but this was different. He had never seen such dreadful damage.

"Don't fail me now, boy!" Locadio cut into his

thoughts. "You panic, and you will go back to your thermopolium for the rest of your days." He was bending over the second man. "Granius! Linen!" he bellowed.

This broke Enecus' reverie, and he moved quickly. He held out the sling of cloth with the instruments in it. "They were boiled less than an hour ago, teacher."

Locadio reached out, taking half a dozen fibulae—the long steel pins used to close wounds—from the cloth. "I'm going to close up this gash. You go to that man"—he pointed to the first man, who was now huddled on the floor, whimpering with pain and shock—"and handle the uvulae the way I showed you yesterday: Cut away any loose edges of skin and then use the gripping clamps to stem the bleeding."

Enecus swallowed hard. "Shouldn't I clean it first?" he asked as he went to the man.

"What's the point until you bring the bleeding under control?" Locadio was already putting the fibulae into place. He looked at the workman, whose face had gone white. "I know it's painful, but it's better than losing blood and ending up with a bad infection. My slave will give you syrup of poppies as soon as I have the pins in place, and then you will get the rest you need."

The man nodded, his jaw so tight that the muscles stood out hard against the cheese-colored skin.

Enecus was trying, unsuccessfully, to pull his patient's hands away from his face. He wanted to shake the man, to get him to understand that he was in

43

danger and Enecus would help him. "Lower your hands," he ordered, but without any ring of authority in his voice.

"By the Twins, boy, be sharp with him! He's counting on you," Locadio said. He had finished putting the fibulae into place and was threading cord through the ends of them to hold them firm. "Hurry up."

Although he was far from certain that this was the best course, Enecus took a deep breath and said to the man in front of him, "Put your hands down. I have to see your face."

To his amazement, the man did as he was ordered.

Enecus leaned forward and stared at the mess the chain had made. His head swam and he felt queasy, but he steeled himself to do as Locadio had instructed him. "I am going to cut away the torn skin. It will hurt, but it must be done." He took the uvula and, using the pointed end, clipped back as many little tags and flaps of torn tissue as he could find. Then he opened the jaws of the uvula and prepared to clamp off the most persistent bleeding. By the time Locadio knelt beside him, he had put three of the uvulae in place and was about to set a fourth one.

"Get that vessel at the side of the nose," Locadio pointed out, "and clip back the edge of the eyebrow." He looked toward his slave Granius. "When you've finished there, Granius, we will need boiled water here, and the herb paste for facial wounds."

"As soon as I am through, master," Granius answered, going on with his work.

44

"The third man has a bad cut on his ankle. I will bind that up, and then I will need your help in correcting the dislocation of his shoulder. For that, we will have to get syrup of poppies. It can be done while he is conscious, but it is better if he is not." Locadio gave Enecus' handiwork another quick inspection. "Not too bad. Get him onto his feet and into the next room. I will have to take some time with his face. Put the herbal paste on the wounds, get a tincture of willow bark down him, and then have Granius prepare for surgery."

Enecus nodded, already struggling to get the man to his feet. "This will be better soon," he said, unable to think of anything else to reassure his patient.

The man muttered something through his torn lips, and it was a moment before Enecus realized that the man had thanked him.

"Well," Locadio said later that evening, "on the whole, you did not do too badly, boy. Next time, you must move more quickly. When men come here in that condition, every instant counts."

Enecus nodded. He was feeling terribly tired, as if he had been carrying stones all day in the hot sun. "I will try."

"I think you will." Locadio poured out a cup of wine and held it out to his apprentice. "If I were one of those high-ranking physicians, I would see that your studies progressed reasonably, that you were exposed to minor duties first—which, for the most part, you are—and I would save such instances as the one this afternoon for later, when you had become more confident. But in a practice like mine, we don't have that luxury."

Once again, Enecus nodded. "Will the men live?"

"The one with the gash will, if there is no infection to waste the leg. The one with the shoulder will be better in a few days, but he will probably have weakness for some time to come, perhaps the rest of his life. But the broken nose, well, he is a more difficult matter, for if there is infection, he might lose his eye at the least, and it could be that the torn skin will putrefy, in which case there is almost nothing that can be done to save him." He drank his wine and motioned to Enecus to do the same.

"I'm worn out," Enecus said slowly.

"Yes. It is often so after such work. In time, you will learn to recognize it. Rest while you can. Drink the wine. I want you to sleep without nightmares, and without a little help from the grape, I think you may have trouble." He poured a little more for each of them. "Tomorrow, who knows what will come through the door? You must be ready for it, Enecus, if you are going to be a physician."

"I *am*," Enecus insisted, but he had to stifle a yawn as he spoke.

At this Locadio relented. "Yes, but perhaps not just at this moment. It's time you were home, boy. Tell that fire-haired sister of yours to feed you well. I will expect you to be ready for more work tomorrow morning. The wounds on that fellow's face must be irrigated— that is, they must be washed out with boiled water, so

46

that the infection may not accumulate in the wound—
and of course, there is much cleaning up to do."

"Of course," Enecus agreed, feeling slightly drugged
with his need to sleep.

"Very good. No nightmares, mind," Locadio said,
taking the cup from Enecus' shaky hands. "Off you
go, boy."

Enecus got to his feet and tottered out into the
warmth of the evening. As he made his way home, he
tried to forget the way the first man's face had looked
as he and Locadio had worked to repair it. For a time,
he succeeded.

By the middle of October, the nights were cooler,
and Enecus had fallen into the habit of his apprenticeship, working in the infirmary by day, listening to
Locadio lecture in the evening, then returning home
to eat and sleep.

"This woman," Locadio explained one night when
they had sent the patient in question home with her
oldest son, "has a disease that we can do little to treat.
She is a victim of the sweet disease, and her girth only
serves to make it worse. The faint she was in today
could recur again at almost any time." He leaned back
in his chair, staring out through the small garden where
they sat.

"But what can you do?" Enecus asked. He was dis-
covering how to pose his questions now, and as a
result, he felt he was learning more.

"First, we can limit what she eats, but that will require

her determination. Then we can provide her with a concentrate of juniper berries, which will help her kidneys to clear her body of poisons. She was awash with water, which made her condition worse. When her bloating is reduced, then we will know better how to proceed."

"Will she be cured?" Enecus wanted to know. He had liked the woman and felt bad that she should suffer so.

"I doubt it, boy. I have never seen a cure in such a case. If she can lose flesh and keep to those foods we suggest, then she will have a chance for some time, but the disease will be always with her. It is not unlike those who become ill at the taste of a single shrimp, but what creates her illness is sweets. It is difficult to tell someone that they must avoid such pleasant tastes." He passed a plate of chopped dates to Enecus. "Here. And while you eat, remember that this woman would have to refuse these."

Enecus took a few of the sweet morsels. "Always?"

"Almost always, or she will faint, as she did today." He fell silent. "It is never easy to know what to advise in these cases. It is not like Demetrius' wife, who has the goiter: All she must do is drink two cups of seawater morning and night, and in time it will fade. It is not like Livinia, who should eat chicken or grains every few hours to avoid the cramp in her side, for if she does this, in time the condition will improve and fade. This is another matter, for there is no way that I have ever discovered to eliminate the disease once it is contracted. It is as tenacious as leprosy, but not as horrible, because it does not cause deformities. There are cases where the fingers and toes become diseased from the sweet sickness, and they must be amputated if infection is not to occur. But once the disease is advanced, there is often little point to such extreme remedies, for the body is then weakened, and it is not easy for the patient to recover from the surgery. Those judgments are the most difficult, Enecus; trying to decide what is best to do. You must measure the immediate advantages against what the remedy might do to your patient's life. In this I cannot advise you—each of us must learn to weigh the circumstances and proceed as best we can."

"But surely, in time, you learn what is best," Enecus said, frowning at the doubt he heard in Locadio's tone of voice.

"It may be," Locadio said as he stared out into the garden again. "But if there is such a certainty, I have not found it yet."

V

"On our way back from Alexandria," Salvius told Enecus as they sat in the dark thermopolium while the first winter storm battered the shutters, "just as we neared Creta, we were pursued by pirates. They boarded one of our ships, but the rest of us got away!"

Enecus listened with a touch of envy. How exciting his friend's life sounded to him! "Was anyone hurt?" The response was becoming automatic, the result of his apprenticeship.

"Well, a few of the sailors were wounded, but nothing serious. Just scrapes and bruises, you know. There's worse every day at the Games." He wolfed down a few more bites of sausage. "But you should have seen the way the pirates maneuvered. No wonder there are rewards for their capture."

"You sound as if you admire them," Enecus suggested.

"Admire them? Of course not!" Salvius paused. "Well, they do manage ships the way no one else does. But that's why they're such a menace, I suppose." He drank more wine and started on his third sausage in a bun. "I've missed this place—and your mother's cooking."

"These days, it's Pyralis who does most of the cooking," Enecus pointed out. "She's been busy with the place since I was accepted as Locadio's apprentice."

Salvius nodded. "How do you like being a physician? Is it anything like you thought it would be?"

It was a little while before Enecus answered. "No, it isn't what I expected. It's harder and it's less certain than I assumed. But it is interesting, most of the time, and . . . oh, I don't know, Salvius. There is so much that even the best physician cannot do."

"Well, I can tell you, trading in cloth is much more exciting than I thought it would be. You should see the cotton merchants in Alexandria. They are all of them thieves, and it takes a wise man to be sure that they do not foist poor goods off on you. There was one man, I can't forget him, who showed us fine goods at his warehouse and then tried to stick us with bales of cloth that were half rotten when it came time to load the ships." He finished the sausage and looked around for more.

"I'll have Pyralis put more on the grill for you," Enecus offered, starting to rise from the stool.

But Mnendos had heard them and he came into the closed room. "Still hungry, are you, lad?"

Salvius laughed. "I have not had good Pompeiian food for more than six weeks, and I am famished for it."

Mnendos set more sausages to cook over the coals. "It's been ten years since I saw Alexandria," he mused aloud, "but I doubt it has changed all that much."

"Well, the Emperor, when he was there, had improvements ordered, and most of them are nearing completion, but you never know what will happen. In another ten years, it may all be rubble." He slapped his hand down on the counter. "Give me Pompeii any day, where things are certain and the world is stable."

Enecus smiled, but his smile faded quickly. "Being a physician . . . it's not like traveling the world to find cloth. About all the cloth we see is the linen that we use as bandages." He stared down into his cup, feeling vexed with himself for being so sullen toward his friend. To take some of the sting out of his behavior, he said, "Forgive me, Salvius; today we had a girl come in, not a day older than you, who had a mortification of her intestines. She was raving with fever and in pain, and there was little we could do for her beyond giving her syrup of poppies and oil of pansy to make her more comfortable. My master told me that had she come to us when the hurt began, we might have been able to aid her. As it was . . ." He could not finish his sentence.

52

"Do you mean she died?" Salvius asked.

"Yes." He helped himself to more wine. "She was filled up with infection. Locadio demonstrated the origin of the problem, but even he said that . . . There are times when the best physician can do nothing."

"Oh," Salvius said, some of his enthusiasm fading. "What do you—I mean, is that discouraging?"

"Of course it's discouraging," Enecus snapped, then once again took a more friendly tone. "You know how you felt when you lost your ship. This was a life that we lost today, and the . . . shame of it is still with me." He signaled Mnendos to give him something to eat. "I am proud to be Locadio's apprentice, Salvius, but I despair at how little can be done."

Salvius considered this, then tried to make a proper response. "Probably you'll get better at it, don't you think? Locadio will teach you, and you will progress beyond him."

"I hope that I will, but there are times that I wonder." He accepted his sausages. "Do not take what I say too much to heart, Salvius. If I had set a broken limb or salved a burn, I would feel otherwise, no doubt."

"Do you do those kinds of things?" Salvius asked, fascinated.

"Well, I help," Enecus said truthfully. "But Locadio is always making me do more things, so that I can learn."

Mnendos handed two more sausages in buns to Salvius. "There you are, you young rascal. If that will not fill you up, you will have to go out into the storm

53

to buy more bread at the bakery; we are running low."

"I will struggle along with these," Salvius promised, winking at Enecus as he bit into one of the sausages.

Enecus did not object when Salvius changed the subject to food—though he had no appetite himself—and began describing all the strange dishes he had encountered in Alexandria.

At the time of the Saturnalia, at the dark of the year, Locadio warned Enecus that there would be more patients coming to the infirmary.

"For most of us, it is a celebration, a way of ending the year with proper tributes for aid and services, as well as thankfulness to the gods for their protection. But it is also a time for feasting and carousing, and you know what that will lead to."

Enecus shrugged. "Indigestion?" he suggested, not quite seriously.

"At the least. There will be those who will gorge themselves and we will have to treat them with purgatives. Then some will eat tainted food, and that will mean there will be sickness that requires great skill to cure. Then, some of them will be far gone in wine and will stumble into things or fall down steps, and their broken wrists and sprained ankles will need attention. A few will be burned from being splashed with hot wine or grease. You will discover that celebrations and foolishness go hand in hand." He folded his arms and looked closely at Enecus. "Were you wishing to have more time with your family?"

"Well . . . uh, yes." Enecus did not like having to admit this, especially with the dire predictions Locadio made.

"I will do what I can. If there are times I am able to spare you, I will. But if Granius or Vibian comes for you, I expect you to return here at once." He shook his head as he listened to the sounds from the streets. "Those who celebrate Saturnalia for all five days often need more than a simple remedy for a hangover."

Enecus could not help smiling. "And come next September, there will be ample proof of that."

Locadio chuckled, but his face was still grave. "I agree with you as far as the babies go, but I am more worried about tainted food and broken heads."

"You said that I have done well," Enecus reminded Locadio, bristling at the suggestion that he was not prepared for his work.

"For an apprentice of less than six months' experience, you have done very well," Locadio allowed. "But that does not mean that you are ready to set a fractured arm by yourself, or to strip the blistered skin from festering burns." He saw the doubt in Enecus' eyes and went on. "We have not yet removed so little a thing as a finger, or opened a skull to relieve pressure on the brain, or cut the disease of the crab from the back of a careless slave. You will need to have done all that and more before you are prepared to go out on your own. And even then," he added more quietly, "you will have many doubts. I have always had them, and I have never met a physician worthy of the name who did not have them."

Enecus realized he had overstepped himself, and he made haste to correct his mistake. "I am sorry, Locadio. I was not thinking."

"That is apparent," Locadio said. "Well, for this evening, since the temples are filled and the banquets do not start until near the middle of the night, go on home. If there is any reason to call you, one of my slaves will come. Keep your dalmatica and sandals near your bed, so that you will not be delayed with dressing." He put his hand on the basket of fruit that Enecus had brought him. "Very nice, this gift of yours. Tell your parents I said so."

Enecus was already starting toward the door, but he turned back, smiling. "I will. It will please them."

"They are fine citizens, your parents. I hope you value them properly," Locadio observed.

"As best I can," Enecus declared as he left his master's house and headed through the dark, windy streets toward his home.

Locadio adjusted the wooden sides to the brace and inspected the broken leg critically. "You were fortunate that this is the worst that happened to you," he said to the young tribune who lay gasping on one of the two examination tables in his infirmary. "That was a stupid thing to do, driving your chariot up the steps of the Temple of Apollo."

The young man had no breath to object with; he hissed in air through his pain-clenched teeth.

Enecus held out the unused fibulae. "Will you need more of these to close the wound?" He was feeling faint from helping with the leg. He had thought he was growing accustomed to the sights a physician faces, but knew that he had a long way to go. From the time two temple slaves had carried the tribune through the door, Enecus had fought the nausea that was building in him. He had never before seen so serious a fracture, with points of bone poking through the skin. Now that Locadio had closed and bandaged the wound, then set the leg and put it in a brace, Enecus had a little better control of himself.

"I will send you home," Locadio was saying to his patient, "and I will have my infirmary slave come to you twice each day, to be sure you have not tampered with the brace. It is emphatically important that you do not touch the brace or the splint or your bandages. You must leave that to me."

The tribune nodded.

"I want you to understand how grave this can be. With all my skill, I am not sure that you will be able to walk without limping. And that is the least you may expect from your folly. If you do not take proper care of your injury, it may fester, in which case you may lose your leg if you are fortunate, or your life if you are not. Do I make myself clear?"

The tribune had turned even paler at this grim recital. He nodded once more.

"Excellent. Now my apprentice will give you syrup

of poppies and then we will bind your leg again. We will carry you to your home. You have told my slave where it is, I believe."

"Yes," he gasped.

"Good. Enecus, get the syrup of poppies. And then clean up. Scrub the floor twice, and be sure that you mix powdered malachite in the water." He looked down at the tribune, shaking his head. "It is bad enough when the gods send us ill fortune, but to pursue it as you did . . ."

Enecus handed Locadio a vial. "Syrup of poppies. I have the linen here, and Granius has started making a sling to carry him in."

"Very good." Locadio took the vial and continued his work.

By the time Granius and Vibian had left with their unconscious burden, Locadio looked exhausted. His eyes appeared to have been burned into his face, and his features were drawn. He motioned Enecus to bring him a chair. "That young idiot," he said as he sat down.

"All those things you said—will they really happen?" Enecus asked.

"Haven't you been listening when I describe these things to you?" Locadio countered sharply. "I will be surprised if he has only a minor infection and several days of fever. It is likely that the infection will enter the bone, which is where the greatest danger lies. If it is localized, then we will open his leg and cauterize the bone to stop the infection. If it spreads, then that is another matter. If the leg mortifies, then, of course, we must remove it." He rubbed his face. "I hope that he believed me enough to be cautious. Young men like that, with rank and money, are often the worst patients. They don't understand what they risk when they damage their bodies." He looked around. "Get me some wine, will you, boy? Put honey in it, and some mace."

Enecus recognized the recipe for a composing drink. "Shall I heat the wine as well?"

Locadio shrugged. "You can see my condition better than I can—do you think that the drink should be hot?"

"Yes," Enecus said after a moment. "You appear to be nervous as well as tired, and so the heat—"

"So you have been listening after all," Locadio said, relieved. "Go on, then. Fill your prescription."

With an odd sense of pride, Enecus went to do as he was told.

Pyralis gave her brother a long, careful look. "You're getting a beard, aren't you? Have you offered at the temple yet? Father will have to pay your beard-tax."

"Three months ago. Before my birthday," he said, smug in this assurance of his emerging manhood. "I shave now, twice a week."

"Ah," she said, laughing a little. "No wonder we see so little of you here."

Enecus frowned. "What do you mean?"

"Well, there must be girls who have discovered you. Doubtless you while away your time in the evening, holding hands and kissing them." Her chin came up

59

as she said this, and there was a bit of an edge to her tone. "That's what young men do, or so everyone says."

"Are you jealous?" he asked, noticing that he had to look down at her. Not only was he getting his beard, he was growing taller.

"Of course not," she said, unconvincingly.

"Well, you may put your mind at ease, jealous or not," he told her as he put his arm around her shoulder. "Those nights I come in late are the nights that work goes late at the infirmary. Last night, when—"

"When you said you would be home for supper, and you were not," she interrupted him. "Mother and I had made chicken with grapes because you like it, and you did not bother to send word that you could not come."

"Will you let me tell you why?" He looked around the storeroom, where she was counting casks of wine and beer.

"It is hardly necessary, I think," she sniffed, turning away from him, her head up even higher.

"Not for you, but for me," Enecus said, dropping onto the stool that was used to reach the highest shelves in the storeroom.

"Go ahead, then, not that it matters," Pyralis said, continuing her counting.

"There was a woman who came to the infirmary, shortly before sunset. She was far gone in pregnancy, possibly seven or eight months, and there had been bleeding that she should not have had. Her color was not good, and she was covered with cold sweat. Lo-

60

cadio ordered that we wrap her in heated blankets, and then he made a potion for her, in the hope that she would not have more trouble than she was already having." As he said this, he found his words carried him back to the infirmary and the poor woman, not more than seventeen or eighteen, her face the same shade as tallow. "You should have seen how brave she was, no matter how frightened. Locadio told her he wished more soldiers had had her fortitude."

"But that did not take long," Pyralis pointed out.

"Not more than an hour, but all the time we had to watch for more signs of blood, or of water. When women have such problems, the midwives send them to physicians, in case it is necessary to take the baby by surgery." He sighed. "It went well, for two hours or so. Her color improved, her breathing was steadier, and the cold sweat stopped. Locadio insisted that we not be hasty in declaring her to be recovered. It was just as well that he did." He rubbed his eyes in unconscious imitation of Locadio. "We had applied warm bricks to her feet and hands, so that she would not take a chill again. It all seemed to be going so well."

Hearing the sadness and defeat in his voice, Pyralis put her tablets down and gave him her full attention. "What happened, Eni?" She had not used his childhood nickname for more than three years; neither of them noticed it now.

"She started trembling. It was just a little at first, hardly more than having her teeth chatter, as if there were a draft in the room. It did not seem important to me, but Locadio said it was a poor sign, and he strove to get her warm." He sighed.

"Did she get worse?" Pyralis asked, knowing already that the woman must have, or her brother would not be as upset as he was.

"Not all at once. She would have a sudden spasm, but it would not last, not at first. She kept insisting that she felt better. That was when Locadio decided to take the blankets off her and examine her. You could tell from the color of her skin, all over the abdomen, that she was bleeding internally. Locadio had been afraid of such bleeding." He clasped his hands together.

"Why was he afraid of it? Does it always happen that way?"

"No." He looked at her. "No, it is very rare, Pyralis. It hardly ever happens. He said that in all the years he has been a physician, he has seen this only twice before. He thought she must be bleeding, because her color had changed and because she was starting to feel euphoric."

Pyralis blinked at that. "Euphoric?" she repeated.

"Yes. He told me . . . oh, months ago, that when bleeding is severe, the patient is often euphoric. Then the patient pays little attention to pain or anything else, because of the wonderful sense of well-being." He took one of her hands in his. "Locadio could not take the baby surgically, not with all the blood, and he could not deliver it the usual way, for fear of making the bleeding worse. So he tried everything else he knew.

It wasn't enough, no matter how we tried."

"Oh, Eni." She wanted to cry, listening to him speak. "If you did all that was possible . . ."

He thought about what she had said. "I think we did. Locadio said as much, when it was all over. We tried everything we could think of. Locadio fought for her. He looked as if he had lost a battle. Well, he had. So had she."

Pyralis hugged Enecus silently, and for the first time in months, she did not resent the long hours he was gone from the thermopolium and from the family. She had known that he would be away from them, but had assumed it would be a simple matter, as it had been when he was taking instruction in mathematics. Now she knew that his life was different from what it had been, and because of that, he had changed. He was no less her brother than before, but he was also an apprentice physician, and that brought an alteration to his life that would be with him forever.

VI

In the middle of spring, Mnendos at last bought his freedom, and to honor this event, Amalius and Rhea gave a two-day celebration. Everyone who bought food and drink at the Gallus Rubeus and knew Mnendos was invited to attend; the street in front of the ther-mopolium was crowded from midday to an hour after sunset with those who had come for the occasion.

"I trust that we won't have any disaster to treat be-cause of this," Locadio muttered to Enecus as they approached the festivities.

"If we do, you may settle it with Father," Enecus responded. He had learned, in the time he had been with Locadio, to answer his jibes with ones of his own.

"You're getting mighty sharp-tongued, boy," Locadio said, smiling.

"I am trying to learn all you teach me, master," Enecus quipped.

"Well, you haven't learned it all yet," he warned his apprentice. "Keep that in mind."

Then they reached the first few revelers, and their banter was forgotten as they made their way to the counter of the thermopolium, each holding out a gift to Mnendos.

"My young master," the former slave cried out, reaching over the wine vats to grip Enecus' wrists. "How it pleases me to see you."

"Keep drinking that Grecian vintage, and you won't see much of anything in a little while," Locadio said, holding out an amphora. "This is from Pola; much better, you'll see."

Mnendos accepted the wine with amazement, for he knew that it was one of the finest made in the Empire. "You are gracious to me, physician, and I have never served you."

"But *I* have served *you*," Locadio pointed out. "I took this rapscallion out from underfoot, didn't I?"

Mnendos laughed loudly at this and turned to repeat it to some of the others who were nearby but had not heard over the din in the room.

"It must be quite an expense for your parents to have such a celebration," Locadio observed to Enecus as they threaded their way through the crush toward the back of the thermopolium.

"Yes, but it is the proper thing to do, and they are so fond of Mnendos, they would do it, I think, for the joy of it, even if it weren't expected." He waved to a few familiar customers, then held up the curtain so that Locadio could enter the family quarters ahead of him.

Amalius was stuffing more sausage into cases, but he put down his work as he caught sight of his son and the physician. "Well, thanks to the family gods, you're here early."

"And may have to leave sooner than we would like, as well," Locadio said, but held out his hand to Amalius, who lifted his palms up.

"Better not. I've got chopped meat and spices and garlic all over me. Let me finish up here, and then we'll greet each other properly." He beamed at Enecus. "It's becoming a rare thing to see you here, my son."

"I'm sorry, Father," Enecus answered.

"You must not be. It means that you are acquiring skills and applying yourself to your profession. We are always pleased that you have time to spend here, but it is fitting that you devote yourself to learning." He went back to his task, packing the sausage meat tightly into the casing. It was warm in the back room, and Amalius was sweating lightly, though he wore only a short tunica and a mantile tied around his ample waist. "My wife is upstairs for the moment, putting on a new stola for the occasion. You will have to compliment her upon it; she took three days to choose this one."

Locadio smiled wistfully. "I recall my wife was much

66

the same way. She was always determined to get the best value for her money, and she enjoyed the looking as much as the buying."

Amalius, who did not know how rarely Locadio mentioned his dead wife, only shook his head and chortled. "It's what makes them so wonderful. Every time I find myself out of patience with my wife, I have only to remember that she takes the same care in stocking our business, and then I absolutely delight in her shopping." He was about half finished with the casing in front of him. "It will be difficult to get all our work done without Mnendos to help out. In time, though, there will be another slave, and we'll manage."

"What is Mnendos going to do?" Locadio asked, hearing a whooping song begin just beyond the curtain.

"Oh, he's bought himself a salesman's license for the amphitheater. He'll be selling sausages on skewers and in buns during the Games. Takes strong legs and a loud voice to do that work, but there's good money in it," Amalius declared. "I did that when I was a boy, to earn a little extra money. I'm not up to it now, of course, but Mnendos is younger than I am, and he enjoys that kind of work."

"It sounds like a strenuous life," Locadio said. "As tough as being in the Legions."

Enecus knew that Locadio was teasing, but Amalius did not recognize the tone, and he gave a serious answer. "I would think it is about the same. But, naturally, Mnendos will cover his ground in the same place rather than tramp the length and breadth of the Empire. Think of all the places the Emperor has been. Not that he'd be up to it now, but still, Judaea, Aegyptus, all the rest of them."

"Very true," Locadio said, and catching Enecus grinning, he patted the boy on the shoulder. "You're pushing your luck."

"You should keep an eye on him," Amalius advised Locadio. "He's unpredictable, that son of mine." He tied off the end of the casing and called out, "Pyralis! The new sausages are ready!"

Almost before his voice fell silent, Pyralis came in from the small garden at the back of the insula where they lived and worked. "I'll take them in and start cooking them." Then she caught sight of her brother. "You're here!" she shouted and hugged him.

"And Locadio Priscus is with me," said her brother after hugging her back.

"How good to see you again," she said, turning suddenly shy.

Locadio said a few proper words, then took Enecus by the shoulder again. "Come. We are intruding here."

"Never!" Amalius protested, though it was true that, with all four of them in the small space, it was difficult for most of them to move without bumping into something or someone.

"You've got to see Mother's new clothes," Pyralis cried out. "Stay here—once you get out there, you'll be overwhelmed."

"Mnendos appears to like it," Locadio said.

"Yes. And it is good practice for later. He'll have to contend with crowds like this all the time." Amalius laughed. "He'll buy his sausages from us, and we've arranged a discount on the price that we would not allow anyone else, and in return for that, he has promised to find us another good cook who is not so expensive that we cannot afford to buy him."

Pyralis agreed at once. "Yes, and the new cook must know more than how to cook sausages if I am to develop a tratorium, with tables and a real menu."

"Listen to her," Amalius said. "Just thirteen and already she is determined to change the business entirely. Well, she is a credit to the family, just as Enecus is, and that is something to give a family real pride. Two children and both of them doing so well in their work."

There was a soft cough, and Rhea came down the stairs, her new stola on display. She said nothing, but managed to do a complete turn in the crowded workroom, smiling at them all.

"It's beautiful!" Pyralis said.

"You're beautiful," Enecus told her at the same time.

"Well, that pleases me very much," Rhea said, her eyes twinkling as she looked from her daughter to her son, and then to her husband. "Well? And what do you say?"

"Oh, I'm no judge," Amalius said. "I am so besotted with you, my love, that you could wrap yourself in woven reeds and you would still be the loveliest woman I have ever seen."

"Which is another way of saying that you never look at a thing I wear," Rhea said indulgently. Then she turned toward Locadio. "You're very patient with us."

"Habit," Locadio joked; only Enecus laughed.

"It is an honor that you come for this celebration," Rhea went on. "We are grateful that you would take the time to do it."

At that, Locadio made a gesture of dismissal. "You place too much importance on a minor courtesy," he said, adding, "Besides, I know how good your food is here, and I could not stay away."

This time everyone laughed, and Amalius offered wine first to Locadio and then to his family, calling out, when it was poured, "May the gods show favor to Mnendos in his new endeavors."

From beyond the curtain Mnendos yelled his thanks in order to be heard over the merriment, then broke into song. Soon everyone within earshot of the Gallus Rubeus joined in for the chorus.

By the beginning of summer, Enecus had learned to set fibulae himself, and to stitch up simple wounds. He could make herbal compounds, extract oils, and prepare infusions and tinctures, and he had two patients whom Locadio had assigned to him. One was a young man who suffered from the wheezing disease. His shortness of breath came on him often, particularly when he was upset, and for that reason, Enecus provided him with oil of cannabis as well as with a compound of comfrey, valerian, hyssop, and nettles that eased the condition. The second was an old woman with swollen and twisted joints of her hands, which he treated with poultices of willow bark and wintergreen mixed with mace.

"I do not want you to assume you're an expert," Locadio told Enecus one day toward the middle of June. "You have much to learn, boy, but you are not doing badly, all things considered."

Enecus was pleased to hear this. "Thank you, master. I did not know you thought so highly of me."

Locadio smiled to hear his own inflection caught so well, but he said more sternly, "You've a way to go before you sharpen your tongue." He indicated a bench by the wall. "You recall the other day when General Quartius Naso Drusus brought his brother to me?"

"Yes," Enecus said, remembering the tall patricians in their silken tunicae, with silver pomanders around their necks. He had rarely seen such high-ranking men at Locadio's infirmary.

"The brother, Sextus Naso Crispus, I knew when we were both with the Cat's Paw. I was his physician then." He tapped his fingers together. "That is why he continues to come to me."

"I wondered," Enecus admitted.

"Yes," Locadio said, hesitating a moment. "Sextus has the falling sickness. There have been others of his rank afflicted with it. Even Divus Gaius Julius Caesar had it, so they say. Sextus left the Legions because of it. He knew it might come upon him while he was leading his men in battle, and he could not face the shame if that should occur. But I was able to give him some relief, and for that reason he has always made a point of letting me look after him. His brother does not completely approve, but he is aware that Sextus has his disease somewhat in check, which is more than you can say for many others with the falling sickness."

"Does he have convulsions?" Enecus asked, recalling a few comments Locadio had made about the disease.

"Yes, and at times they are quite severe. His memory is blank for the time of the seizure as well as for a little of the time preceding it." He sighed. "Sextus is a good officer and it was unfortunate that he could not continue to lead his men. But he did well in leaving as he did."

"You gave him a compound," Enecus said.

"Yes, and I examined him. The compound is composed mostly of mistletoe from Britannia, then lavender, myrtle, amber, and pennyroyal. I examine his eyes, to see if the pupils are equally dilated and open the correct amount. Often you can predict the onset of a seizure this way. I examine his hands and feet for palsy or other signs of trouble, such as discoloration of the nails. Sextus is just a little older than I am, Enecus. He is forty-seven, and you saw for yourself how his sickness has aged him."

Enecus recalled the man's white hair and deep-lined face as Locadio spoke, and he could only agree. "He appears ten years older than you, and . . . weaker."

72

"Yes. It is true that he has lost much of his strength, which is a great pity." Locadio walked the length of the empty infirmary. "It has taken a toll on him, and he will not improve."

"What convinces you of that?" Enecus was startled to hear such unhappy certainty in Locadio's words. "You have often warned me that it is poor medicine for the physician to despair. You've said that where a case is uncertain, it is proper to be hopeful."

"True enough," Locadio said, but without his usual brusque assurance.

"Then what causes you to lose faith in your old friend?" He waited, then dared to ask, "Or is it because he is your old friend."

"Only a small bit," Locadio conceded. "Do you recall the foolish young tribune who ran his chariot up the steps of the Temple of Apollo?"

"Certainly. He broke his leg badly, and you splinted and braced it." Enecus had seen worse injuries since that day, but the impact of that first ghastly fracture remained with him.

"And I warned him then that he would be likely to have a limp at best and could die at worst if he did not take proper care of his wounds," Locadio reminded his apprentice.

"And you sent Granius to attend him each day," Enecus said. "There was some infection, but he is almost completely recovered now."

"That's true. In part because he took what I said to heart. He kept to a simple diet, he did not try to move

73

the leg without assistance, and he sent his body slave to me for instruction. He allowed Granius to irrigate the fibulae twice a day, so that the accumulations of poisons could be washed away, and he kept a good supply of powdered malachite to dust over the injury. He wanted to recover. He was determined to be whole again." Locadio folded his arms and stared down at them, his face turning mournful. "Sextus is not like that young tribune. He is tired of his disease and so he does little to resist it. He takes his medication because it lessens the chance of a seizure, not because it might aid his recovery."

"But do men recover from the falling sickness?" Enecus asked. "You have said that once it is present, it is like the sweet sickness, and it will not leave until life is over."

"True, true," Locadio muttered. "But . . . if a man does not wish to live, there is little a physician can do to prevent his death."

Enecus could think of nothing to say. He knew that Locadio was upset, but there was no comfort he could offer his teacher. He was about to rise, to leave Locadio alone with his desolate thoughts, when the physician began to speak again.

"There is so little we know, when all's said. One man, strong as an elephant, will cut his toe and die of the bending fever. Another will be small, with a twisted back, and he will resist every injury and illness that comes along. A woman will give birth with no more difficulty than a ewe dropping lambs for three or four deliveries, and then be miserable with the fifth." He shook his head slowly. "I wonder why you want to be a physician, when you see how little we can do."

"Because," Enecus said quietly but with great conviction, "I believe it is better to do that little, and do it with all the skill possible, than to do nothing."

Locadio looked up sharply. "How annoying you are sometimes, boy. You go right to the heart of the matter." He let his arms drop to his sides, then beckoned to Enecus. "Come on. There are instruments to boil before either of us can take time for supper."

Amalius paid his monthly fee to Locadio and handed over several small jars of spices. The workroom of the thermopolium was piled high with extra sacks of dried fruits from the summer before, and the space was more crowded than ever. "Pyralis is determined to turn this into a proper tratorium. Already she has expanded our service, so that we have sweetmeat buns and broiled chicken."

"She is a farsighted child," Locadio said, not anxious to get caught up in the workings of the thermopolium.

"Yes." He coughed delicately. "That's the problem. With the money from Mnendos, by rights a portion of that belongs to Enecus." Amalius was feeling embarrassed now, and the color in his ruddy face heightened. "I don't want to deprive my son of what is due him. The law doesn't permit it, and I would not do it, even if it did."

Reluctantly, Locadio said, "But there is a problem." He hooked the leg of a stool with his foot and dragged it nearer so that he could sit down. He had a notion that this would not be the brief visit he had planned.

"Yes. Well, you know how much Pyralis wants to make changes, and that the thermopolium is left to her, in any case. Mnendos has found a slave for sale, a good cook he assures us, young, but not much direct experience. Well, you see, her mother tends the garden and her father is the chief cook for Gerasimus Cucutor."

"Ah!" Locadio said, finding it all much clearer; everyone in Pompeii knew that Gerasimus Cucutor, in spite of his unflattering name, was famous for the magnificence and artistry of his banquets.

"The girl is fifteen, and Mnendos says that she has had the best training in the entire city. Of course, no one knows this yet, and so she's still cheap, and with a bit of skill, I should be able to purchase her at a good savings."

"But that would still mean taking money that should rightly be Enecus'," Locadio finished for him.

"Yes," Amalius admitted. "And that is something I do not wish to do." He dragged a large sack of nuts aside so that there would be room enough for him to sit on the worktable. "Enecus is entitled to his share. That's as it should be."

"But you do not want to deprive your daughter of her opportunity, either." He braced his elbows on the worktable and looked up at Enecus' father. "Amalius

Cano, you have a proposition on your mind. What is it?"

"I've been thinking about it for a few days," Amalius said, still unwilling to come to the point. "I don't want you to assume that this is just a simple dream of mine."

"I will keep that in mind," Locadio said, wishing Amalius would get it over with. "What is your plan."

"Well, you see, Priscus, it's going to be a few years before my boy can take care of himself through his profession, since he's only an apprentice surgeon. You said that yourself not long ago." He patted the table as if it were a nervous animal and might bolt while he was sitting on it. "That means that there is still much that can go wrong and leave him with his training incomplete and little chance to carry it through to the end. Now, we both know that there have been some provisions made, but you never can tell. So I thought that if Enecus is willing, he could be provided a percentage of the business here, instead of his share of the money, so that he would always have an income, even if there are any difficulties later on."

"Of course, the thermopolium might not always be here, or the tratorium," Locadio said, curious to hear Amalius' answer.

"It's more likely that people will stop going to physicians than that they will stop eating," Amalius pointed out sharply.

"Yes, but . . . The city could be sacked by pirates or foreign soldiers," Locadio improvised, enjoying the game.

77

"Don't be ridiculous. The Empire is as sound as anything ever in the world." He glared at his guest.

"Or," Locadio went on, "there might be a terrible plague that kills more than half the people."

"You're making a joke of this," Amalius snorted. "You might as well say that Vesuvius will erupt, and be done with it."

Both men laughed, and Locadio relented. "All right, Amalius, I will tell your boy about the offer. If he accepts it, I will take him into my home a few months early—no harm in that, and it will make your situation here easier. And if it is any consolation to you, I will recommend that Enecus agree to the offer. It will be suitable for all of you to have this business prosper." He got up. "I thank you for getting the spices for me. There are patients who will be far more grateful than I am."

Amalius had been anticipating a lengthy argument and was taken aback when it was over so quickly. "Very good of you," he managed to say as he struggled with his thoughts.

"You will have Enecus' answer in five days. Will that be soon enough, or does this paragon go on the block before then?" He smiled, this time with real humor. "When you buy her, bring her to me. I will tell you if there are any hidden defects."

"You don't suppose that . . ." Amalius began before he recognized the teasing tone in Locadio's voice. "You will have your joke. Well, and I deserve it, keeping you so long."

Locadio gripped Amalius' wrist. "It will be settled soon. Have no doubt of it."

Amalius sighed and waved the physician away, stunned at his good fortune.

VII

In July the weather turned sultry, and because of it, there were more patients coming to the infirmary, men and women and children, all suffering from ailments that were related to the weather.

"We're almost out of juniper-berry paste," Enecus told Locadio while they paused for a light meal in the middle of the afternoon. "I have seen more bloating in the past week than in the whole year before."

"It is to be expected. Any time that the weather is like this, there will be those who bloat. And some will be lethargic. You must be wary of those with the sweet disease and those whose hearts are not strong. They will feel this the most and will need more attention."

The physician was dressed in a pallium, but even that lightweight garment clung to him. "Make sure you are careful about keeping your hands clean. Infection is bred in air like this, and we must not carry it from one to another because our hands are unwashed."

"I have remembered," Enecus said, irritated that he should be reminded after almost a year of apprenticeship. "And I pare my nails every week."

"That's proper. Do not expect me to remind you of something so basic as that." He was drinking pulped fruit mixed with spring water. "You must be certain that you do not neglect yourself, Enecus. It is an easy thing to do when the nights are as hot as they've been. If you do not sleep well, it means that the next day your judgment is impaired, which is something a physician cannot afford."

"I am being cautious," Enecus replied, feeling annoyed at what he knew was an entirely correct reminder. "But it is difficult to get to sleep, and with so many insects, I do not sleep for long."

"I have told you to make a tent of your upper sheet. You will be cooler and the insects will not reach you. There are two boxes of cedar shavings, which you should put around your bed. It will help to keep them off. The Arabic oil, the one that you have used for those with chronic coughing, that will also keep them away."

"I'll see to it." He knew better than to suggest that Vibian be told to do it, for in the time since Enecus had come to live in Locadio's house, the old slave had made it very clear that he considered it beyond his duties to attend Enecus in any way beyond serving him meals.

"Never mind. I'll tell Vibian to take care of it. You will have enough to do here." Locadio looked up as Granius came into the room. "There are more patients?"

"Two, master. One of them has a very nasty cut. He got careless yoking up his oxen this morning, and—"

"And he took this long to get help?" Locadio demanded, unbelieving.

"He claims that he could not spare time from the market. It is a bad wound, master, and I believe the man is in pain." The infirmary slave's tunica was almost soaked through from his sweat. "I need half an hour or so, master. I have not had time to bathe since last night, and you see how I am."

"I smell it, too." Locadio nodded. "Very well. But don't dawdle." He waved Granius away. "Speaking of baths, when was the last time you went to bathe?" he asked Enecus.

"Last night. I spent an hour or so in the tepidarium and did not permit the attendant to use any oil on me." He rubbed his chin. "I was shaved there, too."

"You're up to every other day now, aren't you?" Locadio asked. "By the end of the year, you'll be like the rest of us, with daily bouts with the razor. Still, it helps keep your hand steady for surgery if you shave yourself." He finished his juice and rose. "I don't know what that second patient has wrong, but you'd better come and look at him."

"I will. I have only these dates, and then I am finished." He took one of the sweet fruits in his fingers. "I have heard they canceled the Games that were supposed to take place tomorrow and the next day."

"First sensible thing I've heard in days," Locadio said, approving for once the decision of the magistrates of the city. "The Arena fighters said that in this heat they could not do battle as the crowd would wish, and the bestiarii have complained that most of their animals are half dead already." At the door he had one last remark to make. "Don't think you're that much different from the beasts, Enecus."

When the heat had lasted a week, Locadio had to give himself a day's rest from his work, which left Enecus, for the first time, in charge of the infirmary. He was terrified and exhilarated at once, and he hoped that all he would see during the day was more bloating from the heat and insect bites to be lanced and treated with infection-drawing poultices. For most of the day he had his wish, but late in the afternoon, a slave brought in a man, clearly a prosperous merchant by his manner and dress, who was in the throes of something far more serious than heat prostration.

"He says that his side hurts," Granius told Enecus as he came to the back room of the infirmary where Enecus was mixing up more soothing herbs.

"Which side?" Enecus asked, putting his work aside at once and reaching out for the basin to wash his hands.

"The left." He found a cloth for Enecus to use. "His color is not good, almost gray. He does not breathe well."

"I will need an infusion of foxglove and hawthorn. Mix a moderate solution for the moment, but keep a stronger one on hand." As he gave this order, he was through the door and into the main room of the infirmary, where a pale Thracian slave stood beside a portly man who was struggling to draw air into his lungs. "If you will lie on the table, citizen," Enecus said, using the same tone of voice he had often heard Locadio employ when dealing with afflicted men and women. "I must have a look at you."

"I can't lift my arm," the man wheezed.

"Help him onto the table," Enecus said to the slave. "Do not move too quickly, but do not be slow, either." He glanced at Granius. "The infusion, quickly."

Granius did not hesitate. He was gone at once, leaving Enecus to deal with the patient.

"Do not be frightened," Enecus said as he began his investigation. "What has happened here is that the hot blood and cold blood are out of balance, and the cold blood is pressing on the vessels of the hot blood." Locadio had described the problem to him several times, but he had only seen it once before himself. Now that he had to treat it himself, he found the condition more frightening than before. "The cold blood is slow and torpid, and it keeps the hot blood from giving strength. So you must lie still and permit me to determine how far the congestion has gone."

"You're just a boy," the patient gasped.

"I am Locadio Priscus' apprentice. If he did not believe I had skill enough, he would not permit me to treat you." He was amazed at how confident he sounded, and more surprised to see that his patient accepted him. He hurried about his examination, lifting the man's eyelids and staring at the pupils, comparing the temperature of his two hands, pressing the stomach and chest for indications of obstructions. "Yes, the congestion is advanced. Granius!"

"I am coming!" the slave shouted from the back room.

"I will need the strongest infusion!" Enecus ordered, trying to make it sound as if this were a perfectly ordinary thing to do. "It is on the second shelf!"

"I have it!" Granius assured him and came quickly, holding the glass jar with care. "The measuring cup is on the instrument rack."

"I will want the medium cup. Fill it all the way." He put his hand on his patient's chest, trying to sense the heart action through the ribs. He felt the flutter of breath in the lungs, which alarmed him. "Quickly, Granius!"

"Yes," the slave answered, moving with greater speed now that he realized that Enecus was concerned.

"Lie still," Enecus instructed the patient, wishing he could think of something more original. He watched Granius fill the cup, and as soon as it was ready, he reached out for it, almost spilling it in his haste.

"Careful, lad," Granius warned him.

Enecus had his arm under his patient's neck and was lifting the man's head. "Here. You must sip this. Not too fast." He put the cup to the man's lips. "It does not taste very good, but you must drink it all. It will help you."

Very slowly, the man was able to sip the liquid, and although he coughed once or twice, he got most of the medicine into his mouth and swallowed it. He sighed wearily as Enecus lowered him back onto the table.

"How long, do you think?" Granius asked, being deliberately vague.

"In an hour or so, if he has not shown improvement, we will give him some more. You must keep near him. He is not to be allowed to cough up any of the medicine. He may want to do that, because the cold blood causes the stomach to be upset. If we can bring the hot blood back into balance, then he will live." He whispered the last, so as not to distress his patient.

Granius nodded. "There are three women in the outer room. One of them has a headache, and the other two are feeling ill. I believe it's the heat."

"All right," Enecus said. "Put a screen around this table, so that the women cannot see the man, and then let me talk to them one at a time." He did not want to have his attention claimed by such minor ailments while he had a patient with a congestion of the heart, but he remembered the stern lectures Locadio often gave him on tending each patient with true attention. "For you never know," his master had warned him, "when the most trivial symptoms will mask great illness. It is for you to discover the extent of the disease, not for the patient to guess at it for you."

"Which one do you wish to see first?" Granius asked.

"Whichever seems most in need. If you cannot determine that, then choose the woman who is oldest." He went to wash his hands in the basin, all the while listening for any sound that would alert him to a change in the man's condition.

Two of the women had been reacting to the heat, but the third had a more serious complaint, and Enecus had required more than an hour to treat the woman, and in the end, he had given her three vials of medications with strict instructions as to the order in which they were to be taken. He had been concerned for the woman, who worked as a sweetmeats vendor at the Forum Triangularis on the south side of the city near the two theaters.

"They are to give a play tomorrow," the woman said in real distress. "I must not be lazy when there are customers to buy my wares."

"If tomorrow is as hot as today, the actors will refuse to perform, and you will have no reason to be ready for selling," Enecus countered. "You are not well, woman, and if you persist in keeping busy, you will continue to be unwell until you are truly confined to your bed. If that is what you want, then so be it. But you know that you cannot earn your living from your pillow."

"You physicians are all alike," she protested. "You tell us what to do, but you do not think of how we are to live when we follow your orders."

Enecus put his hands on his hips. "My family runs a thermopolium, and I know what it is to depend on the public to buy your wares. I also know that if you are selling food to the people, you must not taint what they buy. If you make sweetmeats now, it is possible that you will pass some of your infection on to those who buy it. You would not wish your customers ill, would you?"

At that she shook her head. "No. But I do not want to be dependent on charity."

"Would you rather lose the earnings of a few days or of a year?" asked Enecus.

"It's not that serious," the woman said mulishly.

"Not this time. But if it should recur—and if it is neglected, you may be sure that it will—it may be much worse next time." He looked squarely at her. "If you doubt what I say, you may consult Locadio Priscus when he is once again attending to patients here."

"It's not that," she protested at once. "You seem able enough for a stripling. But I also think that you are one who would err in caution. You want me to guard against living. You understand that, do you not?"

Enecus wanted to take her by the shoulders and shake her for her obstinacy. "You are ill. You are able to become well. If you are not willing to make the effort, you must not blame me for your decision."

This cool statement seemed to have more effect on

her than anything else he had said. "Very well. But I will only rest for three days at the most. And if I am not improved, I will return and complain to Priscus."

"I have no doubt of that," Enecus said, not quite laughing. "Do you want me to repeat the order in which the medications are to be used?"

She had sharp, unpleasant eyes, and they glinted at him now. "This, in the green vial, I am to take in the morning and anytime my vision is not steady. This sandstone vial is for taking right after meals, no more than four drops, dissolved in wine or in fruit juice. This last, in the blue jar, is to be taken with bread shortly before I retire to sleep. That's correct, isn't it?"

"Yes," he said, surprised that she had it right.

"Then I can go." She made sure her palla and stola were properly adjusted, then stalked out of the infirmary.

"What a sour creature she is," Granius said from where he was keeping watch over the man behind the screen.

"Yes. Medicine would be easier if it were only practiced on pleasant people." Enecus gave the other two women the prescriptions they had come for, then came to look at the man on the table. "How is he? Is his breathing better?"

"A little, but his color . . . well, you can see for yourself. He has passed no urine since he arrived, and so I cannot tell you the color of it." Granius pursed his lips. "A difficult man."

"An unfortunate one, in any case," Enecus said, his

89

manner mildly distracted. "Do we have fresh orange and lemon peel?"

"What?" Granius asked, startled at this unexpected question.

"Fresh orange and lemon peel—is there any here?" He had just recalled something that Locadio had told him three or four months ago, about the benefits of orange and lemon peel when those with a congestion of cold blood did not respond to foxglove. He thought that Locadio had told him that there were times the citrus fruits were surprisingly beneficial.

"I believe there may be a little. There is some dried, I know." He started away from the table.

"Fresh would be better," Enecus said, feeling more confident now. At least he was doing something rather than standing by helplessly.

"All right. I will see." He went at once to the rear chamber, then came out with a long-drawn face. "No. Whatever we had is gone now."

"Then go to the markets. See if you can buy any. Go as far as the Porta Marina if you must." He reached into the pouch at his belt and handed over two silver coins. "This should get a few of them."

"As you wish, master," Granius said. "If anyone comes?"

"I will manage as best I can until you return." He waved the slave away, then gave his full attention to the man lying on the table. "You will improve, sir. You are going to recover."

The man mumbled a word or two, and Enecus

chose to hear this as agreement while he waited for Granius to return.

"You took quite a risk," Locadio told Enecus three days later when the man was once again himself. "Citrus peel does not always help." He nodded to the patient, who sat half dressed on the edge of the table. "You are fortunate that my apprentice remembered this unusual remedy, and you are equally fortunate that there were ships in the harbor from Byzantium, or we might not have been able to give you any of the peel."

"I will thank the gods for it. Neptune and Apollo, probably." He pulled his tunica back over his arms. He coughed once.

"Are you all right?" Enecus asked, too quickly to reassure the patient.

"Yes. Now that it is cooler, my throat is ticklish, that's all." He studied Enecus from under heavy lids. "You are gifted with fortitude, boy. What is your name?"

"Enecus Cano," he answered at once.

"I am Hyppolytys Niceta. My Thracian slave told me of everything you did while I was at the mercy of the illness." He reached out to grab Enecus' wrist. "Poor man was terrified."

"It is a frightening thing to see one battling a congestion of cold blood," Locadio interjected.

"I have a villa on the road to Nuceria. If I am ever able to be of service, boy, you have only to ask. You have not said, nor has your master, but I am intelligent enough to know that if you had not acted as you did, I would be dead now." He patted his ample middle. "I could feel it here."

"That is quite possibly true," Locadio said, then went on, "but a physician can do no more than the patient will allow."

"Well, let each of us and the gods have his due for my health," Niceta said. "I will take to heart your recommendation to walk in the morning, before the heat of the day. I used to do that, as a young man, but with business demanding so much of me, I have not had the time."

"You will do as you think best," Locadio told him. "But if you wish to keep the blood in balance, you should walk. That way, the hot blood and the cold blood move in harmony through the body. If you venture out when it is too warm, then the cold blood increases to keep you from being taken with sun fever, and we are back where we started. But in the morning, while the air is fresh and cool, the blood rises equally." He held out a small jar. "If you become short of breath or have a cold sweat, then a little of this poured into fruit juice or wine will help you. The fruit juice is better."

Niceta got off the table and accepted the jar. "I will do what I can to keep that in mind." He suddenly braced himself against the table as a tremor, no more than the faintest jiggle, shuddered through the room.

"Old Vesuvius is snoring," Locadio remarked, as most Pompeiians did when the ground shook.

"Well, so long as he never wakens, it's all one to

me," Niceta declared as he finished adjusting his clothes. "You remember that, Enecus Cano. If there is anything that I can do for you, you have only to name it. Send word to the Villa Salicia, and your requests, whatever they are, will be honored. My word on it. And Hyppolytys Niceta is a man of his word; ask any merchant in the Empire."

"You need not say this," Enecus protested, feeling embarrassed to have so much credit given to him. "If anyone is deserving of your generosity, it should be my master—he trained me."

Locadio laughed. "Follow that logic, boy, and the first man to put healing herbs on a wound should get all our fees. Thank your benefactor."

Enecus blushed deeply enough to match his hair. "Thank you," he mumbled. "It is kind of you."

"Not kind at all," Niceta corrected him. "I owe you a debt that no man can pay, and I am not likely to forget that. You could have been lax, or unskilled, or not careful, and that would have been the end of me. You might not be willing to tell me, but I know how close I came to dying, so you will have to bear with my gratitude."

"You make too much of it, sir," Enecus insisted. "It is what I am being trained to do. If I had acted differently, I would not be worthy of my teacher."

"So long as we are handing out laurel wreaths," Locadio drawled, assuming an upper-class accent, "I will admit satisfaction that you acted in precisely the way I have instructed you. Give over, both of you. Much more of this appreciation and humility and I will become ill."

This broke the spell. Niceta chuckled, overpaid his bill, and left, trying not to wheeze as he walked.

"It's all very well to do as you have done," Locadio said when the merchant was gone. "But you had luck in your favor as well as skill. You found the right medications, he was able to swallow them, and the outcome was that he recovered. At another time, it might turn out differently."

Enecus scowled. "Did I do badly, then?"

"No, not badly. It is always flattering to have a patient acknowledge your ability, but do not assume that it means all the credit belongs with you. The patient helped you, and the gods looked on you with favor."

"All right," Enecus said when he had thought about what Locadio had said. "I did not want him to thank me."

"Why not? You *did* keep him alive, boy. Many factors aided you, and you would do well to remember that. But *you* kept him alive."

"But..." Enecus began, then shrugged, too confused to dispute with Locadio.

VIII

All through the summer there were minor tremors in Pompeii. The people living in and around the city took to joking about it with uneasy humor, as if daring the gods of the earth to bring another earthquake on them as they had fourteen years ago. Under the porticoes of the two fora, the citizens congregated to escape the fierce summer heat and to tell one another that they were so used to the earth shaking that they scarcely noticed it anymore.

"I will be grateful to Pluto and all his court if they will refrain from giving earthquakes while I am trying to lance an abscess," Locadio said sharply on a warm and windy August afternoon. The tremor this time had been little more than a wiggle, but it almost ruined his aim. "You are a fool," he went on to his patient while Enecus stood by with cauterizing irons heating in a small brazier. "The next time you get those little thorns under the skin, come to me at once and be done with it. You will spare yourself and me a great deal of unpleasantness if you do."

The patient was a gardener, slave of one of the richest magistrates in Pompeii. He grunted, saying through clenched teeth, "If I came to you for every thorn, I would be here half the days of my life."

Locadio worked to clean the large boil. "You know when you have a serious problem, Gobio, and it is useless to claim otherwise. You are a proud man and do not want to admit that you can be made ill, just as any other man can."

"It's bad enough that you poke holes in me and burn me. Must I listen to you rant at me like a half-wit uncle?" The last few words came out in a rush, and he clamped his teeth together as the little red-hot iron touched his skin.

"You'll get no sympathy from me," Locadio said as he finished cauterizing the wound. "All of this was preventable, and you brought it on yourself by neglect. If you had permitted the infection to spread, there might have been nothing I could do to check it."

Enecus watched how Locadio sealed the wound, thinking that when he had begun his apprenticeship, not quite a year ago, he would not have been able to watch this procedure without feeling nauseated. He still felt a twinge, but he had come to recognize the necessity for the methods, and that made it bearable. "I have the powdered malachite here," he said, holding out the jar.

"Fine. Make sure you get plenty of it in there. We have just got rid of one infection; I have no wish to create another." He stepped back. "Well, Gobio, little as you deserve it, I have taken care of this for you. And if you ever do anything so reckless again, I might refuse to treat you."

"Oh, you'll treat me," the slave said, pulling on his tunica. "You may growl all you wish, but you'll treat me." He handed payment to Locadio. "I will come again in three days. I will wash with water containing comfrey, hyssop, and elder. Do I have that part right?" He moved his arm experimentally, and the skin on his shoulder where the boil had been pulled painfully.

"You'll need a day or two to rest," Locadio instructed him. "If you do not, I cannot answer for the success of the treatment. If that wound opens, the infection will return, and this time it will be deeper in the muscle."

Gobio scoffed. "You're an old woman, waiting for disaster to brighten up your day." In spite of his sarcasm, he did not try to move his arm again.

"And be careful dealing with the hawthorn tree. There is much virtue in it, but it is a plant of mixed blessing. If you do not respect it, you will suffer for it." Locadio turned to Enecus. "Take the brazier to the back room and wash the basin of it as soon as the coals are cool. Put the irons—"

"—to boil with astringent herbs. Yes, I know," Enecus said with an exaggerated sigh. "No need to remind me."

"There's *always* a need to be reminded," Locadio insisted, turning abruptly to Gobio. "That goes for you, as well. And if you have any tansy, bring me some shoots of it."

This last so astonished the gardener that he stared at Locadio as if the physician had run mad. "Tansy?"

"I am in short supply of it. Your master keeps a large herb garden; surely there is tansy in it." Locadio went to the basin by the far wall to wash his hands. "I need more tansy."

"But what for?" Gobio asked in surprise.

"In this weather, there are those who have worms in their guts. Tansy and garlic together do much to get rid of them." Locadio started to tick off on his fingers as he listed the other uses of the plant. "When the teeth are loose or there are sores on the gums, tansy is very useful when applied to the mouth in a paste. There are those with painful joints, and tansy is part of a pain-relieving poultice. When women have their monthly purge, tansy makes the purging easier. Are those reasons enough for you?"

The gardener accepted this. "I will bring you some, when I come back to have you inspect your work."

"I will be most grateful," Locadio said with mock humility. "Now go and lie down for an hour or so. You might not think so now, but you are in need of rest. When the body has been burdened with infection, it requires rest to be strong again. When I was with the Cat's Paw, I saw more men harmed by trying to return to battle too soon than those who permitted themselves time to rest."

"And if my master chides me for shirking my duties?" Gobio demanded. "What do I tell him?"

"Tell him the truth: that you are following my instructions." He was not going to argue with Gobio, that was apparent. "Go. Every moment you waste here is time you might put to better use recovering."

With sudden candor, Gobio said, "I do not want to lie down. If I rest, I will feel the hurt. If I work, it will not trouble me so much."

"If that is your philosophy, it is not surprising that you are in such bad condition. Do as I have told you, at once." He turned away from the gardener and refused to look at him again.

"Your master is a stiff-necked vulture," Gobio complained to Enecus, then shook his head. "All right. I will do as you have ordered. But it is not what I want to do."

Since Locadio would not answer this challenge, Enecus did. "My master knows that, but he is more concerned for your health than your wishes."

When Gobio had gone, Locadio winked at Enecus. "You're learning, boy."

Locadio was busy with a three-year-old child with a congested throat when a young man, about twenty, came into the infirmary.

"Take care of him, Enecus," Locadio called out. "I cannot leave this boy yet."

Enecus was tired, for he had been working since before sunup, when two chairmen had been brought in by the Watch, both of them showing signs of food poisoning. Locadio had set to work on one, Enecus on the other, and it had taken almost until midday for the men to be over the worst of their affliction. Now, with sunset turning the sky the color of new roses, Enecus was ready for a meal and much-needed rest. He did as Locadio ordered, but he did not move with dispatch. "What is the matter, sir, that you come here?"

"Don't be surly, boy!" Locadio corrected him.

"It doesn't matter," the man assured the physician.

"It does," Locadio answered. "But I can't stop what I'm doing to tell you why, just now." He bent over the baby, continuing his work without another interruption.

"I did not mean to offend you," Enecus said with ill grace. "I am not able to see, at the moment, why it is you've come here."

The man tried to make light of it. "It's nothing, really, but . . ." He lifted the hem of his tunica and revealed an inflamed rash on the inside of his thighs. "I thought this would go away, but it hasn't."

Enecus was interested now, in spite of his fatigue. "How long have you had this?" he asked, reaching for an oil lamp so that he would have more light to examine the eruption on the man's skin.

"It's been eight days since I first noticed it. I have

100

been to the baths once since I got it, but the attendants would not let me bathe with the others." He looked ashamed of this admission.

"That's sensible. Others might develop it. And bathing might make it worse. You cannot be sure that water will help." Enecus touched the skin lightly and felt the heat of the inflammation as well as the slight crusting. "You have been scratching this?"

The man shrugged. "During the day, only a little, but at night—sometimes I wake up and discover that I have been scratching. It itches badly."

"I can believe that," Enecus said. "Well, what have you done in the last two weeks that might account for this, do you know?"

"Nothing that I know of." He paused. "I have not gone to any of the women for pleasure. I do not keep a horse in the city, so I have not been riding."

The questions Enecus had just intended to ask were answered with that information, so he peered more closely at the rash. "Have you suffered from the heat?"

"Not particularly," the man said.

"No swelling in the legs? No profuse sweating?" He motioned the man to one of the tables. "If you'll get up here, I'll be able to have a better look at this."

The man did as he was told and did his best to joke about his predicament. "It has not been convenient for me, but it's better than leprosy, I guess."

"Likely" was Enecus' short answer as he had a closer look at the man's legs. "I am going to ask you a few more questions. I'd like you to answer them."

101

"Naturally," the young man replied with a broad smile. "I want to be rid of this."

"Have you been around animals that cause you to sneeze or your eyes to itch?" He did not like the look of the skin, but if the man had been scratching it, Enecus was pretty sure that the condition had worsened more because of that than any other thing.

"No. Not that I can recall." He considered his answer more carefully. "One of my brothers cannot endure cats."

"I doubt that would trouble you in this way," Enecus said. "Have you eaten anything you are not accustomed to eat?" It was the next obvious question.

"Not recently. We had a stew of kid a month ago, when my father slaughtered some of his goats. Do you think that might have—"

"Probably not." Enecus straightened up. "Have you had rashes like this before?"

"No. Oh, rashes, yes, but not like this." He tried to smile again. "It is nothing I am used to."

"Thank the gods for that," Enecus said in an offhand way. "Well, I am going to give you a salve of rue and myrtle. If you treat the rash with it, it should fade in three or four days, that is, if you don't scratch it."

"I will do my best not to," the man said sincerely. "It's driving me mad, and no man likes to be barred from the baths."

"True enough," Enecus said, then went into the back of the infirmary to get a vial of the salve. When he returned, he offered it to the patient. "If you use

102

this up and find you need more, come back and I will see that you are provided with it."

"I am thankful for this, physician." The patient got off the table with care, so as not to aggravate the irritation on his thighs.

On the other side of the room, the baby Locadio was attending began to cry. At once his mother, who had been hovering near the door, rushed forward, crying out in a tone as distressed as her child's.

"Do not be foolish, woman," Locadio said in his most bracing way. "That the babe makes noise is an excellent sign. If he could not get air into him, he would not be able to scream like this, and then you would have cause to worry. As it is, your only concern should be how you are going to get enough sleep with this racket going on."

The mother murmured in confusion, but did not step back. She watched Locadio closely, as if searching for an omen in his face.

"Poor little boy," Enecus' patient said, but without real caring in his voice. "I have a son about that age who is often troubled with coughs, especially when the spring flowers are in bloom. His nurse gives him some concoction or other that seems to take care of him. But still, you would think ... Who likes to see a child suffer?" He took half a dozen silver coins from his belt pouch. "Will this be enough?"

"More than adequate," Enecus said, striving to keep from yawning. "I believe that the magistrates would excuse you a third of that." The prices that physicians

103

were allowed to charge were fixed by the city magistrates within certain flexible limits, but it was not uncommon for a patient to pay more if he could afford it.

"Well, keep it in any case. If I do not recover, I will expect treatment without charge." He cocked his head toward Locadio. "Will you accept my terms?"

Locadio, who had not been listening, said, "If it is fair to my apprentice, then it is fair to me."

"Good enough." The patient walked, rather bow-legged, to the door. "I will see you again in three days."

"You were brusque with him," Locadio told Enecus as soon as the man was gone.

"I am tired," Enecus snapped.

"All the same, you must not be brusque with your patients," Locadio reprimanded him in a mild way.

"Why not? You are." Enecus felt his mettle stung by Locadio's attitude. "You are the most brusque man I know."

"Ah, yes, but I am forty-four, and you are fourteen. I have been a physician for more than twenty years, you have been an apprentice for almost one. When you have had my experience, then you may have my manners as well." He felt the baby's forehead and turned to the mother. "You are to take this child home and bathe him twice a day, adding to the water the infusion I shall give you. You are to place pomanders in his room—I will supply those as well—and you are to see that he sleeps with only the lightest covering possible, so that he will be unhampered in his breathing. I will come to see for myself how he is faring tomorrow evening, and if he has not improved, then I will have to resort to more drastic measures."

"It may be difficult, following your instructions," the woman said quietly.

"Do you think so?" Locadio asked. "What makes it difficult?"

"My husband and I are weavers. We leave our children with his sister for most of the day." She frowned as she said this. "I don't know that she will be able to devote extra time to Antonius."

"Speak to her about the problem. If she is not willing to care for the boy, then I would recommend that only your husband work for a week or so, until the boy is better." He paused, knowing that she was not telling him everything. "Do you worry about your baby?"

"Well, of course. I am a proper mother," the woman said indignantly. "But we have four other children, and we are not rich. If I spend time away from the loom, we will have less income than we must have to feed the others."

"There is the bread dole. You would not starve," Locadio said, in the hope that she might answer his challenge.

"I . . . it would not be possible." She started to reach for the child. "I will do as you tell me, and beg my husband's sister to give Antonius the attention he requires. If she agrees, there is no reason to trouble you again."

Reluctantly Locadio placed the boy in her arms. "He

has been very ill," he reminded her. "If he becomes ill again, I cannot answer for his well-being. Children so young die easily. They are fragile. If he does not die but is sick for a long time, he might never regain his health."

"I will try to explain to my husband," she said a little wildly. "I have part of your payment here. When we are paid for the next bolts of cloth, I will bring the rest."

"When it is possible to pay without endangering the health of your child, then pay me. Until then, spend your money on the boy." Locadio went to the back room and returned with a cloth bag that bulged. "You will find the pomanders in here, and the infusion—it is in a blue jar—for his bath. I have also enclosed some incense to burn in his room when he is not there, to cleanse the air. Be sure you use all as I have told you. It is a pity you do not read; I would write the directions out for you."

She took the bag without comment, holding her child close against her shoulder. Enecus, watching her, had the oddest feeling that the woman was angry with Locadio.

"I will call tomorrow evening. Remember that." Locadio watched the woman and her child depart, his face set in severe lines. "I would not wager on that boy's chances," he said to Enecus. "He was in poor condition when she brought him here. She's half delirious with exhaustion, and if she has to keep on working as well as tend her family, it's likely that she will forget all that she is supposed to do. I wish I had the chance to see the husband's sister. Then I would know more, but I don't like the sound of it."

"Then what will you do?" Enecus asked, rubbing his aching eyes.

"I will visit her, as I have said, and try to determine what is going on." He shook his head as he went to wash his hands. "You might as well clean up, and I'll have Granius set about closing the infirmary for the day. I don't know how you feel, but an hour in a caldarium would be welcome right now." There was a small hot bath behind the infirmary, large enough for three, but not so ample as those marble tubs in the public baths.

"I'll probably fall asleep." Enecus went to wash his hands again, then dried them on a square of clean linen.

"Did you make a wiping of that rash?" Locadio asked as they left the room together.

Enecus slapped his forehead with the palm of his hand. "No. By Venus and Mars! Well, it was hardly that serious. I saw no trace of skin parasites."

"You're gambling with a man's health," Locadio pointed out as he stepped out into the passageway to the street. "I will have Vibian begin supper for us."

For a little while, Enecus felt uneasy about the cursory work he had done on his patient with the rash, but then, sitting chest-deep in the hot water, he ceased to be troubled by it.

IX

There was no doubt that the man's condition was worse, and this time his humor was less pleasant than before. "I used your medication, and see what it has done to me. Three days, and this!"

Enecus turned pale at the sight of the man's legs, for now most of the skin was covered by little crusted eruptions. "I ... I am truly sorry for this confusion," he stammered as he looked in dismay at the infection.

"Confusion?" the man shouted. "There is no confusion here, unless it is your treatment that is confused."

Locadio stepped in to settle the matter. "I can understand your distress," he said smoothly, indicating that the man should be seated on one of the examination tables. "My young assistant has never seen a case like yours, and since the condition closely resembles a far more common ailment, he decided to treat it as he had been taught to do, which is what almost any physician would do in the same circumstances."

The patient shot Locadio a menacing glance. "That is an excellent excuse."

"Of course," Locadio said, hardly raising his voice as he inspected the man's legs, "you have continued to scratch, haven't you? I am sure that my assistant advised against it."

"I can't help it. The thing itches as if there were ants under my skin!" The man was clearly exhausted as well as terribly uncomfortable. "I have lain awake nights and tried to keep from touching anything. But as soon as I fall asleep, my fingers have wills of their own." He sighed. "My mother-in-law gave me a mixture for it, but it didn't help."

Locadio looked up sharply. "A mixture? You used medication other than what my assistant provided?" He managed to sound affronted by this information, which was not often his reaction.

"She thought it would help to stop the itching. Her slaves use it when they are troubled with fleas." He gritted his teeth as Locadio took clean squares of linen and pressed them to the inflammation, then gave them, very carefully, to Granius. "She claims that it stops the itching."

"It must not have done so in your case," Locadio

observed. "Tell me, have you any pets—cats, dogs, perhaps something more exotic?"

"You mean because of fleas?" the man asked. He was puzzled by the direction the questions seemed to be taking.

"No, not precisely. Will you answer my question?" He went to wash his hands, being more methodical than ever as he put his hands into the water and scrubbed them with a rough cloth.

"Well, not pets, but I do come into contact with animals. Would that make a difference?" He was staring up at the ceiling, trying not to watch what Locadio was doing.

"How do you mean? What do you do?" Locadio flung the washcloth into an old barrel, where there were other cloths. "Granius, when you have a chance, change this water. Enecus, don't use it until it is changed."

The patient found this warning alarming. "I . . . what is it about the water?"

"I will explain once you tell me how you come to handle animals," Locadio said gently.

The man sighed. "I am a carter. We transport animals from the quay to the amphitheater for the Games. My contract is with the Master of the Bestiarii. I've handled some remarkable creatures in my time. Why, we've had lions and leopards and tigers, and wild asses and giraffes and elephants, and crocodiles, and serpents four times the length of a tall man. Each one has to be taken in a crate to the cart, and the cart driven from the dock to the circus for the bestiarii to claim. Once in a while, we will take the animals out toward Nola, where the trainers teach the animals tricks, but those are only young ones."

While he spoke, Locadio continued his examination.

"Recently, have you had any unusual animals to handle? Apes, perhaps, or one of the wild dogs?" He called out to Granius, "Is there some of that Hind liquid left, the kind that deadens the skin for a time?"

"I need time to find it, master, and I must do the water first," Granius called out.

"I will find it for you, master," Enecus offered, hoping to get away for a moment.

"No, I need you here, Enecus, so that you may learn to identify these unexpected and rare infections." His tone warned Enecus that there would be more to hear later.

"As you wish. If you change your mind . . ." He looked at the patient. "I am truly sorry that you had to suffer, sir."

"Well, if the problem is rare, I suppose it's natural that you might get it wrong," he admitted grudgingly. "In time, you might be glad you saw my legs, um?"

"It may be," Enecus said, a bit uncertain as to how to go on. "But I would have liked it better if your infection had healed."

Locadio cut in again. "He is a good assistant, but he has not had the experience that I have, and no matter how well-intentioned he is, he needs more time before he can be judged expert." He paused. "About the animals?"

111

"Well, there haven't been many venations recently, but that performer, you might remember him, with all the trained animals? a great Cimri, with a tangled red beard and the build of an ox. He works with bears and wolves and . . . those enormous hounds, as big as a small calf."

"In my profession, I have little chance to get to the Games," Locadio pointed out.

"Oh. Of course." The patient almost blushed. "Well, there is this bestiarius, and I brought all of his animals from the ship to the amphitheater. He let me play with the hounds. Huge, scruffy things, as playful and friendly as kittens. They're so tall, when I tried to straddle one, I could not manage it." He shook his head at the memory. "The only dogs I've ever seen that are bigger are those Scythian hounds, and they are leaner than fence posts."

"A-a-a-h," Locadio whispered. "Big scruffy dogs?" He nodded. "I thought that might be the case." He beckoned to Enecus. "I am sure that when we come to look at the linen, there will be signs of patterns of sores on it, so that we will be able to determine what sort of irritation you have contracted. When the disease is the result of touching animals, you understand, there often are difficulties, because the nature of the animal and the nature of man are related but dissimilar."

Enecus managed to gather enough courage to approach the patient. "I did not mean to cause you any more difficulties," he said.

"Well, at least it won't cost me extra to get better."

The man was not able to smile, but he no longer appeared as forbidding as he had at first.

"I would not charge you for this, in any case," Enecus vowed, blushing once more. "You are not better, and it is my responsibility." Now that he had thought over his sloppiness when the man had come to the infirmary, his shame was growing more acute. "I would not want you to believe that any physician would wish his patient poor health merely to gain a few coins."

"Oh," Locadio said, "there are those who would not have your scruples, but they are not credits to this profession." He saw Granius returning. "Good. Now that I have the solution, I can do something about that itch."

Enecus tried to smile at Locadio, but his expression was rueful. The physician paid no attention to his apprentice as he went to work on the man on the table.

It was more than an hour after sundown, and Enecus sat with Locadio in the darkened interior of the Gallus Rubeus, eating the spiced chicken that Pyralis had cooked in strips on the grill.

"I am sorry for what I did. You are right; I should have taken the time to use the linen." Enecus licked the grease off his fingers without tasting it. "It was wrong of me."

"Yes," Locadio agreed. "I think I mentioned it at the time. But it was only a skin infection, and one that will heal now that the right medication has been provided."

He had been angry earlier, but now his humor was more forgiving.

"And what if it had been leprosy or the crab?" Enecus asked, his conscience stinging him again.

"You would have recognized the crab or leprosy, no matter how tired you were. But your point is well taken. So is this chicken." He looked up. "Pyralis, this is very good. If you are going to add this to the sausages you sell, you will have half the people in Pompeii standing in line at your counter."

Pyralis laughed and tossed her head. She was taller now, nearly as tall as her brother, and her figure had begun to change, so that she no longer looked like a gangly boy. "This is Jocanda's idea. Mnendos was right—she is a treasure, for all her temperament."

"Jocanda is your new slave?" Locadio asked. "The one you wanted to buy?"

"Yes. Father arranged for it, and she's doing well. She is not easy to work with. Last week she threw a jug at my head, but she apologized at once." Pyralis laughed merrily. "When she works out here with us, there are men who come to look at her, because she is pretty and she moves like a tempest coming off the ocean."

"What a pleasant slave," Locadio said sarcastically. "How did you come to buy a creature like that?"

"She cooks like a servant of the gods. We've already started serving her grilled scallops with bacon, just one day a week, and there are those who leave their names days in advance." Pyralis grinned at the two men as

114

she turned to put more chicken on the napkins in front of them. "There are four more strips for each of you. Then you will have to be satisfied or eat else-where."

Enecus did not want to be distracted from his con-versation, but he knew that he owed Pyralis a little attention for the meal she had given them. "You are doing very well, Pyralis."

She nodded. "Thank you for that. I am already half-way to my own tratorium, and our parents have not objected yet. In time I will have it. I will call it *Flam-mia's*, to sound more Roman."

"But Mother and Father ... won't they object?" Ene-cus wondered.

"They did the first time I suggested it, but it isn't as if I am changing my own name, merely naming my business in the Roman manner. They can't object to that, especially since it is good business." She put the last of the strips on the grill. "You can go on with your talk. I will try not to listen. And it won't matter if I do because I don't understand half of what you talk about anyway."

"She's a good girl," Locadio observed as he went on eating.

"Yes." The food was delicious, Enecus was aware of that, but for all the enjoyment he had from it, he might as well have been eating paper. "I ... do you think I should join the Legions, and work with a phy-sician there?" This question was blurted out before his nerve failed him.

"By Juno, why?" Locadio asked, startled at the suggestion.

"Well, to learn more . . ." He saw Locadio frown. "No, I don't mean that you do not teach me well. You do excellently, but I have not been the apprentice I had intended to be. I have been lax in my work, and there are those who have suffered because of it. If I were with soldiers, I would not have that opportunity. I would have to do my medicine properly, and there would be no room for error, or excuse for it." He lifted his chin as if inviting a blow on it.

Locadio put his half-eaten strip of chicken down and sighed as he gave Enecus a long, considering look. "Is that what you have been burning with for the last hour? The notion that somehow the Legions are a better place to learn? That you would be more skilled and more thorough because you are with troops?"

Enecus swallowed hard. "Isn't that—"

"It's nonsense!" Locadio would not let him finish. "Half the time you don't have the medicine you need, or the facilities to boil your instruments without exposing the men to danger. There is no infirmary with a clean-washed floor, only a large tent that swelters in the summer and freezes in the winter, that never has enough light or space for what you have to do. And I have never seen a physician that does better work with the shouts and cries and clash of battle in his ears than he does in a quiet, well-lighted room. You cannot imagine how much more accomplished a physician I am here on Via Palma in Pompeii than I was near an

116

Armenian battlefield." He shook his head. "You worry because of one minor mistake here. Go to the Legions and you will make dozens, and many of them far more serious than this one. Sometimes it will be because you have not the time to spend, sometimes it will be because you do not have the proper supplies, sometimes it will be because the battle will shift and you will have to move men that will die of the handling." He picked up the chicken strip again, but did not eat. He sat, staring hard at his thumbnails. "If I had had the chance to ask for proper learning conditions, I could not have asked for better than what you have with me."

Enecus hung his head. "I did not mean that I would be more skilled, but that I would not..." His voice faded.

"Listen to me, boy," Locadio declared. "You are finally starting to learn what it is to be a physician, and it does not sit well with you just now. Every one of us goes through that from time to time. There is nothing wrong in it. You made a mistake, and you finally understand the ramifications of mistakes. Keep that in mind, and next time it might not be so bad."

"I don't want to make another mistake," Enecus said miserably.

"Who among us does? But do you want to live locked in a room with nothing that might cause you or another person harm for the rest of your life? That will be the only way you can avoid mistakes, and turning away from life and your abilities would be the greatest mistake of all. By Mars, that is why you are an apprentice still. You are learning how to make mistakes properly. With a little good fortune, you will avoid the worst of them."

"I . . ." Enecus did not know what to say.

"Eat your chicken, boy. It's delicious, and you need food in you. Otherwise, you'll be too tired to do your work properly."

Just as Locadio had intended, that last threat provoked Enecus, who started to object, then realized that he was hungry. "All right." He did his best to sound uncaring, but now that his heavy weight had been lifted from his mind, he had no desire to restrain his appetite. As he gobbled down the chicken strips, he caught his sister's eye and made a face at her.

A few years ago she would have tried to pull his hair out for it; now she only laughed.

Late in September the air cooled a bit, and the Games were resumed with more enthusiasm. The cases treated at Locadio's infirmary increased. They ranged from sunstroke to sprained ankles—from rushing up and down the narrow stairs of the stands—to stomach upsets—from eating too much of the food sold at the amphitheater.

Granius had been stacking material for splints when the first of the casualties stumbled through the door toward the end of one afternoon. The man held his hand to a fresh, nasty bruise on his forehead. One of his knees had been skinned and his upper lip was puffy.

"What now?" Locadio asked. He had been tending the boiling of his instruments while Enecus busied himself grinding malachite to powder.

"I need help," the man said thickly.

"I can see that," Locadio stated, leaving his tools to boil on their own. "What happened to you?"

"A fight." He winced as Locadio reached him and pulled his hand away from the bruise.

"I assumed that might be the cause," Locadio said brusquely. "Come over here near the window so that I can get a look at that. Granius! Needle and thread for this one. Be quick about it."

"Do you need my help?" Enecus volunteered, partly out of boredom.

"No," Locadio said, peering at the cut. "I will stitch this wound closed, sir, and then I will tend to your knee. It is the more superficial hurt."

The man shook his head, trying to break Locadio's grasp. "I don't need—"

"You certainly do. What caused the fight?" He nodded toward the blue armband the man was wearing. "That have anything to do with it?"

"Of course not!" was the indignant reply; then he added, "It was the fault of the Reds, in any case. We Blues did not begin it."

"Oh, Mars' Shield! The Reds and the Blues are rioting, are they?" Locadio demanded, completely exasperated. "When will you racing factions learn?"

119

"I said it was the Reds—" the man protested as Locadio shoved him back onto one of the examination tables.

"Anyone but the Blues. And the Reds will say it was the Blues or the Greens or the Whites. Anyone but the Reds! Fools. You stake your whole life on the drop of the praetor's handkerchief, and then you battle like street thieves when you disagree." He had already reached for the basin of clean water that Granius had brought along with the silk-threaded needle. He sponged blood off the man's face. "How bad a fight was it?"

"I don't know," the man said, then yelped as Locadio set the first stitch.

"It will not take long. You get no sympathy from me; you've brought this on yourself, you and the other members of the racing factions." Without warning, he set a second stitch. "You have not said how bad the fight was."

"It was just getting started," the man said, gasping for air.

"God of the drunkards!" Locadio turned away from his patient. "Granius, get the supplies ready. Then go to the Via Marina and fetch that Greek dentist. We'll have broken teeth here soon. Enecus!"

"What's the matter?" Enecus had never seen the calm of the infirmary change so quickly with so little apparent reason.

"We'll be waist-deep in riot victims shortly. I want you to be the one to inspect them. If they have mere cuts and bruises, let Granius swab them and you tend

120

to them when you can. Anything more serious, you decide if you can handle it, or if I should attend to it. I'll need you to help with dislocated limbs. Once that dentist gets here, you can let him handle the teeth." He paused. "Fill up several basins with clean water. Granius won't have much spare time to supply us with water." He laughed once. "Well, you wanted to see what a battlefield infirmary is like—you're about to find out."

As he announced this, two more men stumbled into the entrance of the infirmary, one of them cradling a broken arm against his chest, the other limping badly from no obvious cause.

"Have a look at them," Locadio ordered, and went back to working on his first casualty.

It was after midnight when Enecus finished binding up the last sprained wrist and helped Locadio set the last dislocated shoulder. They sat in the infirmary while Granius and Vibian—sternly disapproving at having to enter the infirmary at all—strove to put the place in a little order before going to bed.

"Do you still want to join the Legions to learn your trade?" Locadio asked while he paused to wash his hands.

Enecus gave a shaky laugh. Now that the ordeal was over, his legs felt jittery and he ached as if he had taken a beating himself. "Not if a battle is worse than this was."

"Not only worse, but it can last for days, or weeks.

Sieges have gone on for years. After a while you believe that no one in the world is whole or healthy." He began to wipe his hands. "We will not open in the morning except for emergencies. Do you hear that, Granius?"

"All the gods be thanked. I will not want to stir for anything less than an earthquake." He was busy washing the floor, muttering at the incredible mess the infirmary had become in a few hours. "Next time there is a riot, may we arrange for them to go to Tarquinus?"

"Not likely. Tarquinus does not like treating messy wounds and bruises. He prefers clients with delicate digestions and an aversion to roses." He motioned to Enecus. "Come on, boy. You look like a guttered lamp. You need your sleep."

Enecus agreed, bowing his head as if his skull were too heavy to carry. "After a while, I hardly looked at them. I saw only injuries."

"A riot, a battle, they're both alike that way," Locadio said. "You did your task well, boy. You have a feel for the work. That's good." He pointed into his house. "Have a little cheese before you go to sleep. It will help."

"I don't think I can eat." Enecus started toward the hall that led to his room.

"Have the cheese anyway. I don't want to have you as a patient tomorrow." Locadio raised his hand and started toward the kitchen at the back of the house.

"Oh, very well," Enecus grumbled, and followed him to get his cheese.

X

Salvius was taller and his shoulders broader. He seemed to fill the entrance to the infirmary, and when he called out, his voice was deeper and more vibrant than before. "There you are!"

Enecus, who was just beginning to wash out an inflamed eye, did not turn at once. The old woman who was his patient was having a difficult time holding still. "In a moment," he called out, not quite recognizing the visitor.

"Too busy for an old friend?" Salvius joked.

As soon as he had finished bathing the woman's eye, Enecus permitted himself the chance to turn to the newcomer. "I don't quite—" And then he realized who had come to visit him, and he gave a whoop of delight.

The two young men thumped each other's backs and howled with pleasure.

"How long have you been back?" Enecus wanted to know.

"I arrived last evening. We had a fast passage, just thirteen days from Alexandria. You will have to come to my father's house and banquet with us tomorrow night." He grinned, but beneath this satisfaction, Enecus thought there was an apprehension.

"If Locadio doesn't need me, it would be my pleasure," Enecus assured him.

"Fine. Wonderful." Salvius looked around. "So this is where you work?"

"Yes. And I must do a few more things before I can spend a little time with you. Granius! I will need a paste of malachite. I want this woman to anoint the lid of her eye with it."

The old woman cocked her head to one side. "Make me look like a foreigner," she complained.

"Better that than a blind Roman," Enecus said seriously.

She was chastened by this warning. "Yes. Much better."

"Aren't you being a little harsh with her?" Salvius asked in an undertone.

"No, not really. She's been here before, in as bad condition, and she does not like to use her medication. The trouble is that every time the infection recurs, it makes her eye that much weaker." He put his hand on the old woman's shoulder. "I do not wish to see you here again for some time, Iona. Do you hear me?"

She nodded. "Yes, young physician. But you ask a lot of an old woman."

"No more than your eye requires to stay well," Enecus said firmly. "It is not enough to smear some of the paste on at night for a time or two and think that will suffice. You must wear the paste day and night for more than two weeks. Is that clear?"

Her smile was crafty. "I am old. I do not remember well."

"But for this you will do as I tell you," Enecus insisted. "I cannot be responsible for your vision if you will not use the medication."

"That's not what your master would say, boy," the old woman said in a saucy way, shaking her old gray curls as if she were sixteen again.

"My master would say much worse to you, and you know it well," Enecus responded. "Take the jar that Granius gives you and make sure that you use it as you have been instructed." He helped her off the table. "Come again in three days. If I do not see a marked improvement, then Priscus will speak to you."

The old woman muttered as she took the little jar, but she did not argue as she left the infirmary.

"Where *is* your master?" Salvius asked when they were alone.

"He is visiting a patient with a fever. It's a sad case, and he is baffled by it. I cannot blame him for his feeling. It is galling to think that there are diseases and maladies that no physician can treat." He crossed his arms. "I have to wash up, and then I will take you to the thermopolium. My family will want to see you as much as I do."

"Your master leaves you alone like this often?" Salvius wanted to know while he watched Enecus clean his hands.

"It's a pretty recent development, but in the last month or so, he has been more willing to do it." He dried his hands, then called out, "Granius, I am going with my friend to the Gallus Rubeus for a meal. If anyone arrives who needs urgent help, send Vibian for me."

Salvius fell into step beside Enecus as they left the infirmary. The afternoon sun poked long golden fingers down the narrow streets, gilding the paving and touching the houses with light. "I've missed this place," Salvius said. "Even the sight of a proper biga can make me homesick." He pointed to one of the small two-horse chariots trying to push through the crush of pedestrians. "Look at it. A biga is the finest vehicle on land, I swear by every god in the pantheon."

"You *have* been gone too long, if that turns you lyric," Enecus teased him. "You haven't decided you like the exotic places better?"

"Well, there are some things that can only be had in other countries. There are fabrics and foods and women that defy description. You may think that bringing them here is enough, but it isn't. There is a smell

126

in foreign places that is like nothing else on earth. Just as Pompeii has its own smell."

They were almost at the thermopolium now, and in many ways it felt to both of them that no time had passed. But there were other indications that it had, and it was not only Salvius' short, neat beard that marked the difference.

"My sister is making changes," Enecus warned Salvius as the two of them came in sight of the awning.

"She's always been adventurous," Salvius remembered. "I hope your father marries her well."

"Father has not had an offer that I have heard of," Enecus said.

"He will. I . . ." Suddenly Salvius seemed awkward and he hung back. "That banquet tomorrow night. You have to come."

"If there are no patients," Enecus promised, puzzled.

"It is . . . because I am to be married," Salvius said in a rush. "In January. My . . . bride is coming from Byzantium. It is . . . all arranged." He turned quite red under his tan. "You must be there. I'll sink through the floor if you don't come."

"Married?" Enecus said, not certain he had heard correctly.

"Her family are silk dealers in Byzantium. They deal with the merchants on the Silk Road." He stared at the thermopolium. "What has Pyralis been up to?"

This change of subject was too much for Enecus. He laughed heartily. "You'd better come and see be-

127

fore we're both so confused that neither of us knows what the other is talking about."

It was only the second time in his life that Enecus had had to wear a toga, and he shared heartily in the general dislike of the cumbersome garment. He lay on his banquet couch, swathed in fabric, and tried to free his arm enough to reach for some of the sweetmeats that the slaves were passing to the guests. He was used to his pallium for special occasions, and thought that it was sufficiently formal, but his parents and Locadio had been adamant about the toga. He wished he had not let them talk him into it.

"The last toast of the evening is to the happiness of the betrothed couple," Salvius' father said. He was not very steady on his feet, and the words came out slurred, but the guests obediently took the fresh cups of wine and drank the toast.

Salvius, reclining on the couch next to his father's, was looking a trifle pale, and his eyes had the glaze that told more than wine cups did how much he had drunk. "She's a good girl," he called out, as if repeating a lesson.

The formalities were almost over, and Enecus was glad of it. He wanted a little time to talk with his old friend, and though he did not know how capable Salvius would be of making sense, he did not want to miss the opportunity. He accepted a date stuffed with almond paste as the flute players entered the room to provide entertainment.

A slight tremor shook the place, splattering wine on the littered floor. One of the guests, no longer sober, fell onto his well-padded backside and the others laughed.

"Old Vesuvius cares little for dignity," Salvius said, and the company laughed.

Enecus was relieved now that he had drunk so little wine. It had been Locadio who insisted upon it. "For I will not have you trying to treat patients while your head is throbbing and your eyes are red," he had informed Enecus as he prepared to leave for the banquet. Earlier in the evening, Enecus had felt vexed by this order, but now he knew it had been the best decision.

"I want to talk," Salvius said to Enecus. He had made his way, a little uncertainly, from his couch to Enecus'. "I won't have much time tomorrow or the next day."

"All right," Enecus said, a bit uncertainly.

"You're thinking that I should wait a while. I'm not old enough." He belched and sat down rather abruptly on the end of Enecus' couch.

"I don't know. I know that *I* would not want to marry yet. I can't afford it, for one thing. And I have not been about the world as you have." He sat up, tugging at a trailing bit of cloth from some part of his toga that had somehow got unwound.

"Still." Salvius signaled for more wine, then thought better of it. "I want to clear my wits," he told Enecus. "So you think you haven't seen enough to marry, is that it? I'd say you've seen more than I have, at least of women."

"In one sense, yes. But taking care of a disease is not the same thing as knowing a woman for . . . what she is." He cleared his throat. "You know more of that than I do. I know it."

"Perhaps," Salvius said, adding, "They say that physicians have all kinds of women, anytime they want them."

"Only if they're ill," Enecus quipped, wishing Salvius would not dwell on it.

Salvius stared up at the ceiling. "I've met my bride. Pretty little thing, very dark hair, all in curls, cut short. Comes no higher than my chin."

"Do you think you'll mind being married?" Enecus asked.

"I don't know. I don't know what it's like to be married. It's nothing I know about." He rubbed his nose. "Her father and my father are pleased with the match, and Venus knows I've seen uglier women. And I'm not all *that* young, I suppose." He got up. "Still. Still, I didn't think it would be so soon."

"It is strange," Enecus agreed. "But your families want to do things to your benefit. It makes for bad business if you're not comfortable together." He had heard this argument many times, but until now he had not thought much about it. "She has her own wealth."

"About the same as mine, and I understand there are other monies willed to her. She won't be a burden on me, or I on her. And she's just two years older than I am, which is reasonable. It's close enough."

"Not unreasonable," Enecus said.

"I guess I'll be more used to the idea in a month or so." Salvius frowned. "I don't mean I don't want to marry. That's not it. But I didn't think . . ."

When he did not go on, Enecus finished for him. "You did not think it would be so soon. Yes, you said that." He started to rise. "It is very late, my friend."

Salvius grabbed Enecus' elbow. "I'm still not sure that this is how I want to be living, ten years from now."

"You won't be," Enecus said, chuckling. "You will have children and a house of your own and you will be wondering what to do about your children's future instead of your own." He had been told that by his father not more than a week ago, and while he did not doubt it was true, it troubled him to think of it.

"Well, I will have to talk to you more, but not now. I ought to be more sober when I talk about life, oughtn't I?" He took a few lurching steps toward the door. "The footman will arrange for the Watch to light you home."

"I can find my way," Enecus said. "The Watch know me now. They've seen me at all hours when I've had to visit patients." He finally found two ends of cloth and tied them together so that he would not trail the material on the street. "Treacherous garments, these togas."

131

Salvius followed him to the door. "I am glad you came. I'll make more sense in a day or so."

Enecus repeated all the proper thanks that good manners demanded, then gave Salvius a gentle poke on his upper arm. "You can do the same for me, when it comes time for me to marry."

"A pleasure," Salvius said owlishly and bowed his friend into the night.

A few days after Salvius' wedding, when a blustery winter storm hooted and slapped along the sea between Sicilia and Pompeii, Enecus found Granius in the rear room of the infirmary, smearing a drawing paste on his badly scraped knuckles. "What are you up to?"

Granius almost dropped the earthenware container at the sound of Enecus' voice. "Oh! I thought you were—"

"Locadio?" Enecus ventured. "What is wrong with your hand, Granius?"

"Nothing. Nothing important." He tried to conceal it, but Enecus reached out and drew it toward him. "You don't want to bother yourself over my hand, Enecus. It's just a scratch."

"Like the writing on all the walls of Pompeii?" Enecus said lightly. "That's the excuse for those things, too. Let me look at your hand." He pulled the reluctant slave toward the window. As the cloud-dimmed light fell on Granius' hand, Enecus raised his eyebrow in surprise. "That is not a simple scratch, Granius. How did you come to get it?"

The slave sighed. "That chairman, the one with—"

"You mean the one with that dreadful infection?" Enecus had grown hardened to many terrible things in the time he had been Locadio's apprentice, but he could not recall without a shudder the chairman with a wounded foot so filled with infected matter that it was the size of a large melon and smelled worse than a privy.

"Yes. I went three days ago to change the dressing, and, well, I'd scraped my hand. I know you're not supposed to treat infected wounds when your hands are cut, I *know* it means taking a chance, but don't you . . . Enecus, I was in a hurry. It had to be done, and so I didn't take all the precautions. It was stupid, that's true, but I didn't mean for it to be like this." He stared down at the red and puffy areas on the back of his hand. "I've got to get this taken care of without my master finding out. If he ever learns of this, he'll sell me for sure." Granius looked up swiftly at Enecus. "You're not going to tell him, are you?"

"I ought to, Granius," Enecus answered carefully. He was studying the infection in the hand. "How long has this been reddened and swollen?"

"A day, no more than two. It wasn't bad until this morning. Before having my fruit and toasted cheese, I soaked it in hot seawater, just as you had the chairman soak his foot. And I don't have any of those dark

133

lines running up my arm the way they ran up his leg. It will get better, Enecus." His eyes narrowed. "You'll take care of it for me, won't you?"

The temptation was enormous. Enecus started to refuse, then said, "I will tell you what: I will look after it for three days. If it isn't worse, then I will continue to treat the hand, provided you will not object to my informing Locadio. He has many tasks for you to do, and you cannot very well do them with a hand that is diseased." He thought for a moment longer. "I will tell Locadio that you have scraped your knuckles. That is the truth, if not completely accurate. That will make it possible for you to take better care of your hand and not pass the infection on to others. And you must give me your word that you will soak your hand in hot seawater at least three times a day."

Granius was so relieved at this offer that he could hardly find the words to say so. "You are a good man, Enecus, and you are going to be a fine physician, and I will do precisely what you tell me."

A year ago, Enecus might have set great store by this avowal, but he had seen enough of patients' disregard for their physician's instructions, so that now all he did was give a grunt to indicate he had heard. "What have you been putting on it, other than the ointment of mandragora to kill the pain?"

"The malachite, and myrrh," Granius admitted. "It's helped a little, but I need . . . rest."

"If you're willing to tell Locadio what happened, I am certain he will be willing to let you rest. But if you

134

do not tell him, then you must not expect him to help you that much." Enecus glanced at the window. "At least it is chilly. In hot weather, this would be far worse than it is."

Granius nodded, as if he needed to agree with everything Enecus told him. "But the hot seawater? Isn't that correct?"

"Oh, yes," Enecus said confidently. "That's entirely correct. There might be some advantage in using the willow bark paste on the scratches after you've soaked your hand next time. I think it will lessen your discomfort." He sniffed at the infected area. "The ailment has not taken hold yet, and it's not too difficult to keep it under control if you'll do as you are told and not assume that you are better than you are."

"I won't do that. I don't want to lose my hand. It could come to that, couldn't it, like the chairman almost lost his foot." For the first time there was real panic in the slave's eyes, and Enecus knew that he had to soothe him.

"This is not nearly as bad as the chairman," he said candidly. "For one thing, you do not walk on your hands." Ordinarily Granius would have chuckled, but now all he did was stare into Enecus' face, hoping for encouragement. "And you have not tried to bind up the scratches all the time, which would only serve to make them worse."

"I knew that was wrong," Granius said at once, eager to show how much information he had garnered in his work.

"That's something to be thankful for. Burn incense at the Temple of Apollo tomorrow, and ask him to work on your hand." Although Enecus was not sure that he put much faith in the intervention of the gods, he had discovered recently that a patient who could do something—anything—toward his recovery was likely to do better than one who felt entirely helpless. "I will expect to see you before you go there and when you return."

"Fine. Yes. I'll do that at once," Granius said. "I mean, as soon as I have finished my work in the infirmary." He was babbling but did not care. "You are a king among physicians' apprentices, Enecus."

"I hope you will think the same of me in a week's time," Enecus said with a show of humor that he did not feel.

XI

Shortly after the mild quake rumbled and shuddered through Pompeii, one of Salvius' slaves rushed into the infirmary, a message in his hand. "Is the one called Enecus here!" he shouted.

Locadio, who was righting the nearest overturned basin stand, straightened up and regarded the new-comer quizzically. "Why do you want Enecus? Won't I do?"

"My master, Salvius Valens, sent me for Enecus Cano. He says that it is necessary that Enecus come at once." The slave was breathing deeply and he appeared nervous. His clothing proclaimed him to be one of the storeroom slaves that many of the cloth

137

merchants owned. "There is an injury."

"Your friend Salvius wants you," Locadio called out, then explained to the slave. "He's in the rear chamber with my infirmary slave. The stupid fellow needs his hand bandaged." He raised his voice. "Enecus, you'd best hurry."

"Very well!" Enecus called back and appeared shortly after that, pulling a second woolen tunica over the one he wore. "It's still cold outside," he explained to Locadio.

"Fine. Keep warm, by all means. You're not much use to me if you get sick." He looked at the slave. "Did Salvius Valens say why he needed my apprentice?"

The slave nodded at once. "There has been an accident," he said. "There are injuries."

"Then you'd better take your tools. Mind you've enough splints," Locadio told him. "I will not expect you for a little while."

Enecus was already checking the small wooden chest that contained his tools. He closed it and threaded the leather straps through the slots cut for them. This left him with a length of leather to serve as a shoulder strap. "If there are problems, I will send word to you."

"It's not necessary." He thought a moment. "But *I* will have Vibian inform your parents that you will dine with them later this evening. It will give them a chance to see you, and the cook will not be kept waiting on two meals here." He patted Enecus on the shoulder. "You know how to take care of most accidents. If there is anything you have doubts about, send word and I will come to lend you whatever aid I can."

As he followed the slave into the streets, Enecus asked, "Where are we going?"

"To the mercers' emporium, by the Porta Urbanis," the slave said.

This was almost clear across the city, and Enecus looked startled. "Shall I call for a chair?"

"We'll be faster on foot," the slave said, and looking at the traffic in the narrow street, Enecus had to admit that he was right.

"Then perhaps we should move more quickly?" Enecus suggested, trying to peer through the tangle of people and bigae and handcarts that jammed the way. "The Via Legati is faster, isn't it?"

"Possibly," the slave said, but he did not take the cross street that led to it. "I was told to come this way," he explained.

Enecus knew better than to argue the point, although had the way been more crowded than it was, he might have insisted and taken the responsibility for his decision. "How many are hurt?"

A street vendor with several long sticks holding ring-shaped pastries jostled past them, his face rigid with fatigue.

Enecus reached out and tugged the man's arm. "How much?" he asked, pointing at the pastries.

The vendor was prepared to haggle, but he saw the urgency in Enecus' expression, and so chose a reasonable price. "Two for five quadrans."

"Fine," Enecus said, fishing the coins from the pouch on his belt. "Four of them."

The vendor hooked the four off the longest of the poles and handed them over with expert speed. "The gods will smile on you," he promised. "These are the best in all Pompeii."

"Naturally," Enecus said, taking his pastries and following the slave once more. He offered one of the pastries to the slave, then began to consume the others. "I doubt I will have much chance to eat for a while."

The slave blinked. "How can you endure food when you know that you will have to see terrible things and—"

"I couldn't a year ago. But Locadio Priscus has taught me well. If I am hungry and tired, I will not be as alert as I must be." He nodded toward a red-painted notice on the side of the building across the street, announcing: *Jupiter, the Biggest and Best, showers favor on our Emperor, Vespasianus.* "They say he's coming here next month."

The slave shook his head. "I cannot read, master."

"The Emperor is supposed to come here. The sign praises him." He had seen the Emperor only once, when he was ten and his family had gone to Roma to see Amalius' brother. Enecus had stared in amazement at the Emperor Vespasianus and his two sons, Titus and Domitianius, as they rode at the head of the Praetorian Guard through the Forum.

The slave said nothing. He ate his pastry and kept walking.

By nightfall, there was only one casualty for Enecus still to treat. Four of the slaves had been battered by stacks of collapsing bales of cloth, many of which were as heavy as a good-sized man. In many ways the one who was left was in the worst condition. On Enecus' orders, the slave was carried on a stretcher to one of the counting rooms on the side of the emporium.

"What do you think?" Salvius asked as the two of them walked toward the counting room.

"The break is a bad one, and there are bone splinters I will have to take out before I can set the arm. How much damage has been done I am not sure, but if I were you, Salvius, I would find other work than this for that slave to do." They reached the door of the counting room, where a large number of oil lamps had been brought.

"I have been boiling the tools," the slave who had brought Enecus to the emporium said, and he pointed to the basin of hot water. "That is ready for you, too."

The injured slave lay on the clerk's writing table. His face was ashen and his skin was clammy to the touch. His left arm was stretched out, so that the break was visible.

"It is a shame that he was trapped under the bales for so long," Enecus said to Salvius. "It has made matters worse, because he has lost much hot blood, and the cold blood has made him suffer this way." He set his case down and took out a pair of spectacles with thick lenses. "These will help me to see the smallest splinters, Salvius. Otherwise there will be pain and infection when I set the arm. There may still be pain and infection, but it will be less." He signaled the slave to bring his tools and as soon as he had washed his hands, he set to work, taking care to be as gentle as possible.

"Why is he so docile?" Salvius asked as he watched Enecus tweeze a long shard of bone from the exposed muscle.

"Well," Enecus said in a soft, remote voice—his attention was on the injury, not on Salvius—"he has suffered a great deal and fainted. But I have given him a light dose of syrup of poppies. It relieves much."

"There are those in Alexandria and Byzantium who use syrup of poppies as others use wine. I never tried it; watching them frightened me. But I tasted hemp flowers two or three times. I felt I was floating." He looked around the room, trying not to see what his friend was doing to the slave. "My wife's brother is one who loves the hemp flowers. His father has threatened to disinherit him if he continues to indulge his appetite for them."

Enecus made a noise to indicate he had heard Salvius, but he had given little attention to the man's words. He had encountered this pattern before. Often patients would be accompanied by a friend or family member who was compelled to talk while the patient

142

was being treated. He had learned in the last year not to let this distract him. While Salvius rattled on, Enecus found the last of the fine bone splinters and, with the aid of the spectacles he was wearing, removed them. As he straightened up, he could feel how stiff his back had become. "Slave," he called out. "Those little pins, the fibulae there: Boil them for me. I will need them for closing the wound."

"Are you finished?" Salvius asked anxiously as Enecus set the spectacles aside.

"This part is finished, yes. But there is more to do. First I will have to set the bone, then I will have to close the skin with the fibulae and twine, and then the wound will have to be irrigated before I splint the arm and bind it in a sling." He went to wash his hands before the next stage.

"I never . . . You do this as if you have been doing it all your life," Salvius declared.

"There are days that I think I *have* been doing it all my life. But I am not all that advanced, not really. You should see what Locadio can do. He would have had the splinters out in half the time it has taken me. And he can put in fibulae like a weaver at the loom. I saw him work on an injured mason once. The man had fallen from a scaffold where he had been building a wall, and he was in far worse condition than this poor fellow. Locadio had him in splints and braces in less than an hour. I was astonished." He wiped his hands with care. "I wish I had Granius here, but I can manage alone."

"Who is Granius? Why do you want him?" Salvius asked sharply.

"He is the infirmary slave, and he is good at holding the patients while bones are set. I will have to put my knee against his chest while I align the bones in his arm. Well, no matter. It's a bit slower, but it works as well." He turned to the slave. "Are the fibulae boiled yet?"

"Just now," he said. "I'll get them out for you."

"Take care. I don't want to have to dress burns as well as broken bones." He said it easily, but he could sense the apprehension in the slave. "You have done very well, and you deserve much credit." He took the fibulae and resumed his work.

Pyralis had grilled oysters for Enecus and Salvius, and Jocanda had made a dish of cold cooked grains tossed with onions, chopped carrots, sliced hard-boiled eggs, and pine nuts with vinegar and olive oil. "She is a treasure, no matter how difficult she can be." Pyralis grinned at her father, who had come in from the rear room to have a cup of wine with Enecus and Salvius. "You've admitted it at last, Father."

"Yes, I'll admit that vixen can cook, but she is almost more trouble than her talents are worth when her temper is raging." He looked at Enecus. "Your mother is the only one who can talk sense to her when she becomes enraged. I wouldn't have the nerve to approach her."

"But if this is any example of what she can do,

144

then . . ." Enecus shrugged and ate more of the cold grain salad. "You're looking prosperous, Father."

"Well, and so I am. We all are. In another year or so, if all goes as we hope, Pyralis will have her tratorium and this thermopolium besides. You'll see your investment flower yet, Enecus."

"That would please me," Enecus admitted. He looked over at Salvius. "Do you want to invest in Pyralis' tratorium?"

"When the time comes, I might be willing," Salvius said, quite seriously. "The improvements here are impressive." He drank more of the wine. "Is it like this every day, Enecus?"

"You'd have to ask Pyralis," Enecus said.

"No, I don't mean that. Do you always bind up injured limbs and set broken bones and . . . all the rest of it?" He stared down at his plate. "I was watching you very carefully."

Enecus leaned back. "Most of the time there are children with coughs and sniffles and men and women with sore joints and unsettled stomachs. There are those with insect bites and loose teeth and misshapen toes. But there are other ills, too, and many of them are worse than what you saw today. Some of them I have never actually seen, but Locadio has told me about the conditions and explained how they are treated. One or two of them I hope I will never see." He picked up one of the grilled oysters and ate it eagerly. "There are days it is almost boring, and there are days when it is so harrowing that I think being chained to an oar

145

on a bireme would be preferable. But it is my chosen work, and I do not regret my choice."

Salvius snorted. "When you said you wanted to be a physician, I thought you'd gone mad. I could not imagine why you would want to stay here and do nothing but tend to the ill and infirm. I was sure it was all a waste of time, and a foolish thing for any enterprising youth to do." He drained his wine cup. "And I pitied you for all you were missing. I saw myself going about the world, adventuring, not as much as I wanted, but it was better than—"

"—tending the ill and infirm?" Enecus prompted.

"Salvius!" Amalius chided him.

"I didn't think. I just didn't think about what it meant. I never thought that being a physician meant more than that. I thought of that old Greek sham who attended my grandmother, and I thought it was always like that." He looked at Enecus, almost defiant.

"Why didn't you say something?" Enecus asked.

"Because I was ashamed that my friend should want to be such a thing." His voice fell to a mumble.

"As if Enecus could be like that!" Pyralis exclaimed.

"Well, how was I to know?" Salvius asked truculently. "I thought he wanted a safe life, and who is to blame him for that?"

"You were, it seems," Enecus said, but with a grin. "Come, Pyralis, fill the cups again, or he will be afraid that I no longer like him."

Pyralis did as she was told. "You're a bigger idiot than I thought you were, Salvius, if you truly believe that this is the way my brother—"

"Now, Pyralis," Enecus interrupted her. "He hasn't finished, and I want to hear what he has to say, not to listen to the two of you argue."

"Yes, give him a chance to say the rest," Amalius seconded. "You perturb me, Salvius. I would have thought you were more astute."

"Well, that was two years ago," Enecus said, giving his friend an excuse.

"That was part of it, I suppose," Salvius said, grateful for this chance. "But I just didn't *think*. But today while I watched you, I almost wanted to trade places with you, except that I know I could never do what you do." He dared to look Enecus in the face. "I could have done nothing for that slave, no matter how much I wanted to, and if I had tried, I would certainly have made it worse."

"You can't be sure of that," Enecus said, wanting to spare Salvius the distress he clearly felt.

"Oh, yes I can. These last two years, I thought I was the clever one, the fortunate one, the courageous one because I go all over the Empire buying cloth and trading for goods. I thought that made me better and wiser." He drank some of the wine, his cheeks turning red, more from embarrassment than drink. "Well, it doesn't and I'm not. I have nerve enough to bargain with a Persian and get the better of him, but I can't stop a good slave from needless suffering if his arm is broken. You were as calm and unruffled as . . . as Pyralis there at her grill. You handled men I could

147

hardly bring myself to touch, and you cared for them no matter how troublesome they were."

"You needn't dwell on it, Salvius," Enecus told him. "It is how I earn my living. You think that I am calm—well, I'm not, but I have learned how to be. And I could no more bargain with a Persian than sprout wings and fly." He clapped his hand on Salvius' shoulder. "Leave off, now. You're making my sister dismal, and if she is dismal, Jocanda will have to cook, and she'll probably empty the wine casks over our heads if what they say about her is true."

Salvius allowed himself to be convinced by this. "May the gods spare us that!" he cried out, and asked for another grilled oyster.

"There," Enecus said to Granius as he inspected the slave's knuckles carefully. "It looks as if there is no more infection under the skin, and the scars won't be that bad. Flex your fingers for me."

Granius did as he was told, bending his fingers with great care, as if they were made of glass. "Well?"

"Are they painful?" Enecus asked, wanting to be sure.

"Not really, just stiff." He moved them again, this time more easily. "I think in a day or so, it will be better." The smile he achieved was not really happy, but he no longer looked as careworn as he had been. "I am grateful, Enecus."

"As well you should be," Locadio said from behind them.

The two young men turned, both of them startled, one of them frightened. "Master," Granius whispered.

"Those knuckles healed up at last, have they, Granius?" Locadio asked, a bit too indulgently. "Sure they're all right?"

"Excellent," he muttered.

"And you, my apprentice? Do you think his knuckles have healed well? Considering how badly infected they were, of course." He waited while the other two exchanged glances.

"How did you find out?" Enecus asked, making no attempt to deny what he had done.

"There were bandages, Enecus. The smell of them was enough to tell me that you were treating more than a mere scrape. What was the cause?" He looked from his apprentice to his slave. "Are you going to tell me, Granius?"

"I . . . I made a mistake."

"By which I assume that you got pus on a scrape and did not immediately wash your hands in herbal water." He did not need to have his guess confirmed. "And then you compounded your error, didn't you? You took no precautions after the first mistake, so that by the time you started to treat the infection, it had got a hold under the skin. Would you say that I have the general picture?"

Granius lowered his eyes. "Yes."

"Of course, you preferred to have my apprentice attend you," Locadio went on.

"Yes!" This time Granius was not humble. "He knows

how to do his work and he would not read me lectures like—"

"Like this one?" Locadio suggested sweetly, then turned to Enecus. "Nothing to say?"

"Only that I tried to convince him to talk to you, and he would not do it. Rather than let the hand go untended, I agreed to take care of it." He met Locadio's gaze directly. "You were the one who said that I should learn to use my judgment."

"Yes, I did." Locadio folded his arms. "And what do you think of your judgment? How is my slave's hand?"

"Your slave's hand has healed. Look at it yourself, if you wish. Under the circumstances, I think my judgment was satisfactory. I would have preferred that you treat your slave, but as your apprentice, I have an obligation to help you, haven't I? And caring for your slave is part of the obligation. Isn't it?" He was aware that if Locadio were truly furious, he would have ripped them up by now, and so he took courage and went on. "You have instructed me in caring for these infections. If I could not help your slave, what right would I have to treat anyone else?"

"Don't bandy words with me, Enecus," Locadio said severely, though there was a gleam in his eyes. "You're getting too sure of yourself by half."

"You have told me that a physician should do his best to appear confident, so that the patient will not be afraid." Now he grinned openly. "If I have done something wrong, rebuke me."

"A lot of good it would do," Locadio responded.

150

"Well, Granius, how do you evaluate Enecus' treatment? Did he give you proper care and did he prove worthy of his calling?"

"He did very well," Granius said, trying to appear as at ease as Enecus did.

"And what of the risk you took? What of the danger you were in, Granius? You were not authorized by me to be treated for illness of any kind, and this man did not have permission to treat you. You endangered not only your health, but your physician. Under the law, I could sue him for harming you." Locadio waited in the silence.

"But he did *not* harm me, and he is your apprentice, and . . . and there was never any question about my health, because *you* trained Enecus, and there is no better physician in the Empire than you are." This outburst startled Granius more than anyone else, and he looked around in some confusion when he had finished.

"Granius, you're subtle enough to be a Greek. What sort of a man would I be to resist flattery like that." Locadio shook his head and relented. "You were both wrong, and the gods favored you more than you had any right to expect. But who am I to fly in the face of the gods?" He indicated the outer room of the infirmary. "I believe we have patients that need our help."

Obediently, Enecus and Granius went to work.

151

XII

All through the spring there were occasional tremors, and the citizens of Pompeii stopped paying much attention to them, for none of them were very serious. Since little damage was done and hardly anyone suffered because of the minor earthquakes, politicians made jokes about them and vendors in the streets danced when the earth shivered under their feet. Occasionally household slaves complained when crockery was broken, and those who lived in the poorest insulae had to endure little showers of plaster when the cheaply constructed walls cracked, sending lines through the rooms in strange designs, as if a giant hand were scribbling there.

"Bad omens," Vibian muttered when he served a late supper to Locadio and Enecus. "They have said that the leopards at the amphitheater have refused to mate, and that is ominous."

"For you, a midday cloud is ominous," Locadio countered. "Find me a real portent and I might put some stock in your doomsaying." He spat grape seeds across the room. "I love the summer. Fruit for three months, and apples in the autumn. Fruit is good for health, be certain of it. Better good fruit than too much pork."

Enecus laughed. "From a man who almost lives on pork buns, you're a fine one to speak."

"Well, at least I know the risks, which is more than you can say of most of the rest of them." He shook his head slowly. "A poor excuse; you need not remind me, Enecus. We'd all of us do better if we ate with care, but who wishes to, when pork is so good, and the fried breads are sweet?"

"Not I," Enecus admitted. "But you've said that we like what is beneficial to us, Locadio. If that is the case, then pork and fried breads are excellent for everyone."

"Yes," Locadio said. "But do you know, I've come to think that we are given those hungers by the gods so that we may learn to appreciate them, and use them in moderation. Wine is a pleasant thing, but a man who is corrupted by drink is not. The wine is not corrupting, but the man is corrupt. Another man is undone by eating so much honey that the teeth fall out of his head and his body becomes so obese that he cannot move without wheezing like leaky bellows. It is not the fault of the honey that the man cannot stop himself from eating it." He leaned back on his couch. "I must be getting old, turning so philosophical at mealtime."

"It's a pleasure to listen to you," Enecus said honestly. "Your memories of your days with the Legions have taught me a great deal, and this . . . you remind me that we are all fallible."

"Fallible?" Locadio scoffed. "Oh, the charity of youth! Spare me from it, one of you gods." He laughed heartily and was not troubled by the little earthquake that accompanied his own outburst.

Vibian's omen arrived at the end of June: the Emperor Titus Flavius Vespasianus had died of a severe chill at Aquae Cutiliae.

Pyralis baked the proper funeral meats to sell during the official week of mourning and endured Jocanda's constant complaint with good humor. "It's surprising she should be so displeased," she told her brother as they waited to sign their names to the city rolls of those honoring the new Emperor. "She has said for a year that the old man should die and let the young rule; now that he's done it, she's infuriated that she cannot try out her new way of making chicken and scallops on the grill."

Enecus was tired from a long night. "Vespasianus wasn't all that old, just sixty-nine. There are many older men."

"But they don't wear the purple, do they?" Pyralis

asked as the line moved a few steps closer to the civic podium.

"I don't know. Galba was older, I think." Enecus had more on his mind than Emperors, and it galled him that he had to take the time for this event.

"And you know how *he* ended!" Pyralis reminded her brother. "Otho made sure he died."

"Otho was a young man, and he fell before summer," Enecus countered. "I only hope we don't have another four-Caesar year. Think what that would mean for the Empire."

Pyralis chuckled. "And think of the lines we would have to stand in."

At last he relaxed. "Oh, all right. I'll stop grousing. How's the thermopolium? Are you still pleased with your choice?"

"Yes!" She clapped her hands. In the last year she had grown almost as tall as he, and her body was rounding into a more womanly shape. "I don't believe you truly wished to give it to me, but I do not regret my choice, not at all."

"Fine." He sighed. "Titus Flavius Vespasianus, father and son. Do you think Titus will want to change the coins now he's Emperor?"

"Of course. They always change the coins," Pyralis said, trying to sound as worldly as she could. "So long as they don't devalue them again, it will be good that they mint more."

"It was unfortunate that the Senate authorized debasing the silver." He could not forget the fury with which Locadio had expressed himself when he learned that the silver coins were to be stamped with base metal in them.

"It won't be so bad," Pyralis said, determined to be cheerful about it. "Our parents aren't that worried." She looked around, as if searching for friends in the line. "They signed the roll yesterday. They stood in line most of the afternoon."

"Oh, fine," Enecus said sarcastically. "Does that mean it will take us that long? I warn you, I haven't the time to spare."

"Who does? Mnendos was furious. He kept saying that at least slaves didn't have to put up with this foolishness." They advanced a few paces more. "But at least we have time to talk. There has been so little time, Enecus."

"Yes. I'm sorry I did not come last night," he apologized, knowing he had disappointed her. "There was a woman in labor, and it was difficult for her. The baby had twisted, so that it could not deliver properly. It was three hours before we were able to bring him around to the right position, and by then she was so exhausted that we were not able to do much for her."

"Is she all right?" Pyralis asked, her eyes becoming wide with amazement.

"No. She died just after dawn. We gave her herbs and massaged her body and placed her in a warm bath, but it was no good." He bit his lower lip. "It is not always so difficult—may the gods be thanked for it."

Pyralis stamped her foot, her newly found prettiness making that gesture charming instead of petulant. "I *hate* it when you tell me these things. I don't *want* to know about how people die. I want you to tell me about how you save them and make them well again."

"I would like that, too," Enecus said, trying to make light of it.

"Then why do you trouble me with these tales?" she wanted to know.

"Because it is a pleasant, easy thing to make a patient well, and see him be healthy. That is when I take pride in what I do. When we save someone, then I do not question my choice of profession. But when there is nothing I can do but watch as the patient suffers and dies, then I curse myself. It is hard to do, Pyralis. There are times when all I can think about is how helpless I am, and how terrible it is that the patient must endure pain and indignity for no reason. There was a patient brought to us not long ago who had been bitten by a mad dog. When that madness takes hold, no physician can be of aid. We made the poor man as comfortable as he could be, and made sure that he was not left alone. When he died—it was not very long in coming, but at the time I thought it was months—he had been so tormented that he welcomed the end. And for his sake I welcomed it for him, too, so that he need not suffer again. Yet at the same time, I was infuriated that I had been able to do nothing but keep him from harming others and himself while the madness ran its course through him."

157

He stopped and squinted up at the sun. "Then I wonder if I have been a fool and should learn to be a boatwright or a chandler or a fisherman, and leave the unfortunates to others who are more able to stand the work than I."

Pyralis had listened to him reluctantly, but when Enecus was quiet, she put her hand on his arm. "Who, other than you and Locadio, would you trust to care for me, if I fell ill?"

Enecus looked at her, startled by her question. "Why do you ask?"

"Because if you can think of no other, then you know that in spite of everything you've told me, you have made the right choice."

Enecus heard this with real surprise. "You . . . you're getting very skilled, my dear little sister."

She gave a playful slap to his shoulder. "Is that all you'll allow me? *Is* it?"

He ducked her hand. "All right, I'll admit you've given me something to think about."

As she advanced in the line once more, she shot a look at him over her shoulder. "You're turning out proud as a Persian navigator." Then she gave her attention to the various announcements painted on the walls around them and refused to talk with him again.

"The smoke is a good sign," Vibian insisted on the second day. "They say as long as Vesuvius is smoking, it will not erupt."

Granius made a rude sound. "Very fine, but what

158

are we to do with those whose heads and eyes ache from the smoke? There have been half a dozen slaves in the infirmary this morning who cannot work because their throats are raw from breathing the stuff." He emptied out the basin he carried, then went to one of the jugs to refill it. "Tell the master that, and see what he says."

"He has not lived here for very many years," Vibian reminded Granius in a superior tone.

"Nor have I. And if that means I still have sense enough to get away from a volcano when it's smoking, then good for me." He held the basin with care. "The master says that he expects to be working late tonight. Do not prepare supper until an hour after sunset. He also asks that you go to the Gallus Rubeus and get half a dozen sausages in breads for him."

Vibian stiffened at this. "If it is his wish."

"And bring some of that chicken back for me," Granius added. "I haven't had anything since my morning cheese."

Vibian glowered at the younger man. "It is not proper for slaves to order food without the permission of the master."

"Oh, for the patience of Attis," Granius burst out. "We have been treating half the city for running noses and stinging eyes since first light, and I'm getting hungry. Bring me food from the thermopolium or make it yourself. I would have thought you'd prefer being free to run errands and to assist our master, but if you would rather not, it is all one to me."

"Well, I will get extras, in case they are necessary and I am short of time to do the cooking." It was as much as Vibian would concede.

"Excellent," Granius said, and sneezed violently. "The smoke is affecting me as well as the rest of the city."

"Have the master give you an elixir for it." Vibian assumed a superior attitude. "I have been more fortunate than you."

"Yes, if you do not suffer from the smoke. And the noise of the thing!" He made a rude gesture. "Rumble, rumble, rumble, thunder, growl, that's all the mountain has done for two days. I'm getting tired of it."

"It will stop in time. It always does." With this as a parting last word, Vibian left Granius alone.

Amalius held a torch to light his way to Locadio's house. When Vibian finally answered his knocking, he said, "I realize it is late, but I must speak with my son."

Vibian was tired; his old eyes were red-rimmed from irritation brought about by the smoke from the volcano. He wanted nothing more than an uninterrupted night of sleep, but he behaved properly, standing aside and reminding Enecus' father to enter the house with his right foot. "Enecus is dining," he said when Amalius was inside and the door bolted once more. "The green chamber. You'll see it as you cross the atrium."

"The gods thank you," Amalius said, handing Vibian a copper coin as token before starting toward the room.

Both Locadio and Enecus were at supper, devouring the last of a baked fish and stewed pears. They looked up at the sound of footsteps, Locadio swearing quietly at the interruption. When he saw who it was, he relaxed. "I trust you are not here with some complaint. We have had more patients today than I have seen this side of a battlefield on a single day."

Amalius drew up a bench and accepted the cup of wine Enecus held out to him. "No, I haven't any trouble with my health, if that is what you mean. Other matters worry me, which is why I have come."

"Are my mother and sister well?" Enecus asked, sensing the depth of his father's concern. "Has the smoke harmed them?"

"Not especially, no. Certainly no more than it has harmed most of the people of Pompeii." He drank half the wine. "I sent them to Nola this afternoon. I told them that I wanted them to get out of the smoke before it made them ill. They took Jocanda with them, as soon as we finished serving the midafternoon crowd. I want them to stay away until the skies clear again."

"That's a sensible precaution," Locadio remarked. "Old Vesuvius has been in a surly mood. As soon as the smoke stops, it should be well again. Although the magistrates will have to authorize a fresh coat of paint for the public buildings. Everything is covered in soot. I've been told it's worse at Herculaneum."

"Well, with the wind out of the east, what would you expect?" Amalius asked. "At least we're to the south of the mountain; they're due west."

"We're to the south," Enecus pointed out. "We might not have so much smoke, but it's denser, which is why

161

so many suffer while the skies are filled with it." He ate a little more of the fish. "Even the food tastes of it."

"They say that the catch has been poor the last two days. The fish are going out to sea." Amalius drained the cup. "Ah, that was good. I have been on my feet for most of the day, packing things and serving in the thermopolium. Your sister"—he turned to Enecus— "is mad as fire. She did not want to leave, and when I insisted, she almost went to the magistrates to be exempted from a parental decision. You can thank your friend Salvius for changing her mind."

"Salvius?" Enecus asked, startled. "I thought he was in Massilia, buying wool."

"He came back day before yesterday, and found the smoke. His family has been loading up carts, emptying out their emporium so that they can keep the cloth clean. He has negotiated for storage space in Caralis."

"On Sardinia?" Locadio laughed. "Isn't that going a bit far?"

"Well, Salvius' father thinks there is going to be an eruption, and he does not want his goods damaged. He wants to put the Mare Tyrrhenum between him and Vesuvius." Amalius accepted more wine. "If worst comes to worst, and this smoke keeps up, I gave Rhea my word that I would take passage on one of Salvius' ships, as he offered. Your mother, Enecus, is a very prudent woman, but you know that makes her cautious, as well." He wiped his hands on his tunica. "I cannot remain much longer. I don't like leaving the thermopolium unattended. With Vesuvius smoking and the ground trembling, robbers are everywhere. You'd think the mountain infects them in some way."

"It might," Locadio allowed.

"There is one more thing," Amalius said awkwardly. "I'd like very much to keep in contact with you, Enecus, until this unpleasantness is over. I would like to think that if there is trouble, we would not be separated."

Enecus felt a sudden surge of love for his father. He rose and clapped his arm around Amalius' shoulder. "You honor me. But my place is here, for as long as Locadio requires me. I am his apprentice, and I must not turn away from him simply because times are difficult."

Amalius hugged Enecus with rough affection. "No, you're not one to do that." He cleared his throat. "Well, do not let the day go by without word from you, or I will worry, and I have enough on my mind without that." He started to leave the green chamber, but was stopped by Locadio.

"You may believe that I will not ask your son to take senseless risks, Amalius," he said quietly. "He may not be as valuable to me as he is to you, but I do not hold him worthless, either."

The two older men exchanged a significant look, and Amalius nodded. "Very well. If you decide to leave, let me know what gate you use, and where you are bound." With a last grip on Enecus' shoulder, he left the room.

"You are fortunate in your parents," Locadio observed when they had finished the meal in silence.

"I know," Enecus said, emotion making his voice husky.

# XIII

Another day went by with no improvement. Vesuvius bellowed and sent up clouds of stinking smoke, and even the hardiest of Pompeiians stopped joking about the mountain. At the infirmary, Locadio and Enecus treated lines of patients who came with conditions ranging from the most mild of coughs to full-blown asthmatic bronchitis. There were also those with varying degrees of skin irritations and inflammations like bee stings.

Locadio kept his doors open for treatments for more than two hours after sunset, but finally exhaustion took its toll of him and Enecus, and he told Granius to turn away those who were waiting. He had started to rasp when he spoke, and it was not only fatigue that changed his voice. "Pernicious smoke," he muttered as he went to wash his hands. "My eyes feel as if they've been burned into my head."

Enecus nodded, not looking up from the drying cloth. "How many, do you think?"

Granius, who had kept count, answered, "One hundred forty-two adults and fifty-five children."

"Mars and Apollo!" Locadio said with feeling. "Too many. How did we . . . Never mind." He sat on one of his examination tables. "Tomorrow, if the volcano is still smoking, we will have to leave, I think."

"What?" Enecus turned in surprise. "This morning you were saying that you would not be scared away by an ill-mannered mountain."

"That was this morning," Locadio reminded him in a dispirited tone. "I have had time to reconsider my answer." He wadded up his drying cloth and tossed it toward a basket that was already filled with them. The cloth fell two paces short of its target. "Much more of this smoke, and I will need treatment myself. You are not able to manage all this alone—no one would be, so do not glare at me that way, Enecus—without collapsing from the work, even if the volcano was not active. If we remain here, we make ourselves worse than ineffective. If we leave the city, as so many others are doing, then we stand a chance to aid others in their plight as they leave. That woman you treated last? She must leave the city if she is to live. Her lungs are

166

congested now; another day of this and she will drown in her own fluids."

Enecus listened with growing apprehension. "There must be another way, Locadio. We are obligated to help those who suffer."

"If that's what's holding you back," Locadio said acidically, "remember that tomorrow there will be many leaving the city with us, and at least half of them will require the aid of physicians. You will have more than enough chance to succor those who have been hurt and are ill." He got off the table. "You'd best get some sleep before you fall over."

Enecus started to object, but then chuckled. "You're right. It's all I can do to speak, let alone think." He rose. "In the morning I will send word to my father and gather my supplies. What we will tell those who come to us for help, I dare not consider."

"We will recommend that if they are troubled by the smoke and the noise to leave the city for a short time, until it is safe to be here." Locadio signaled to Vibian. "Tomorrow morning, we will need to know which gate is best to use and if there are arrangements to be made with the Watch. I will leave it to you to settle the matter before we arrive at the gate." He coughed twice, his face changing color from the effort. "I will expect to be awakened just after first light, or at whatever time there ought to be first light. With all the smoke we might as well be at the bottom of a pit." He started toward the atrium, then paused. "Just get this place in some semblance of order. There's no sense in scrubbing the floors, not with that soot everywhere. Put the instruments to boil. That will be sufficient." He stared at the bench where Enecus had been sitting. "I wonder if we should take a few household items with us as well?"

"It will not be necessary, or so the magistrates have said." Granius was already preparing the pot to boil the instruments. "But I will take all the medicaments from the back room, so that looters will not be tempted to use them."

Vibian, who had come at his master's signal and was not about to return to the other side of the passageway, held the door open for Locadio and Enecus. "They say that the women of pleasure have agreed to leave the city tomorrow afternoon, when the play has finished."

"If *they* are leaving the city, then it is a good precaution for us to do so as well," Locadio declared. "When a woman can't sell love, a city is doomed indeed." Chuckling, he went toward the atrium, yawning once, then coughing again.

Amalius looked up as his son came into the storeroom. "What's the matter?"

"Vibian was too ill to come, so I wanted you to know that Locadio and I will be leaving soon. The Watch is not letting people out through the Porta Nola—the theater is filling up for the play and dancing, and the streets are too jammed—so we'll be leaving through the Porta Nuceria. We should be ready to leave within the hour. I hope you'll come with us." He realized that he was being too abrupt, but he was pressed for time and too tired to take the time to argue.

"Just like that?" Amalius asked testily. "No consideration for what I might want to do?"

Enecus shrugged. "Father, you are wrong to remain. They say that the volcano will not erupt after so much smoke, but the smoke is very bad for you. Since you've sent my mother and sister out of the city, you cannot pretend you're ignorant of the danger." He saw the stacks of wine kegs by the door. "Or are you leaving?"

"Tomorrow," he said. "I agree with you, but at my age, it takes more than smoke to get me out of a place." He folded his arms. "Still, to have you take time to come here, it does my heart good, my son."

"You're my father," Enecus said gently. "I worry for you."

"And you are growing up. There was a time when it was only the parents who worried, but when you reach a time when the children worry in return, you know that they have ceased to be children." He sighed. "You haven't time for a little wine, I take it?"

"I'm sorry. I have other errands to run before we leave, and Locadio is not well enough to do all of them himself." Enecus hesitated. "The city is very crowded, what with the play and all. Don't wait until the last minute to leave, if you think it's wiser to leave before you are quite ready. Leave the supplies, if you must.

We can always buy new supplies, but lives and good health are irreplaceable." He went to give his father a swift hug. "Remember what Salvius said. Go to him if you must."

Instead of arguing, Amalius simply nodded. "I'll keep that in mind. And I'll send word along the Via Nuceria to find you if you aren't back in the city by the first of September."

Enecus knew he was expected to laugh, and for that reason alone he tried to appear lighthearted. He took quick leave of Amalius, then hurried along the streets toward Salvius' house. The sky was dark overhead, and although it was early morning, very little light penetrated the black, stinking clouds that billowed out of the volcano. Enecus felt in need of a bath, as much to cleanse the soot off his skin as to end the constant sting he felt from the sulfur in the air.

Salvius had to be summoned from his private quarters, and Enecus paced through the peristyle as he waited, cursing the delay. When Salvius came at last, Enecus was short on patience. "There you are."

"Enecus," Salvius said. "What's the matter? Is there trouble?"

"There may be," Enecus answered, realizing that he had alarmed his friend. "Locadio and I are going out of the city for a few days until the smoke clears a little. My mother and sister have already left."

"Yes, so I was told," Salvius cut in. "I was pleased to hear it."

"And I," Enecus admitted. "But my father is still

here, and he does not want to leave with me. So I have come to ask you—if you take to the water, will you send a slave to bring my father? He is a stubborn man and might remain here longer than it is safe." He had not intended to speak in such a rush, but once the words began, he could not stop them.

"I can't seize him like a convict," Salvius said reasonably.

"No, of course not. But you could remind him that he will not find another boat he is sure of getting aboard. That might make a difference. He is stubborn but he is not a fool." He gave a long, searching look to his old friend. "Well?"

Salvius nodded. "Certainly. But I warn you, we are planning to take to the water by midday. We have one of our shipping vessels waiting at the marina, and the captain is under orders to be away at noon."

"Fine. If you can spare a slave in an hour or so . . . ?"

"Yes. I have a young man from Toletum in Hispania I can spare. He should be able to persuade your father to join us." He gave a tight, unhappy smile. "I would go myself, but I must attend to the household."

"Yes, naturally," Enecus said, hastily preparing to leave. "You may find me in Nuceria if this goes on much longer. We leave this morning." He grasped his friend's wrist. "Be safe, Salvius."

"And you, Enecus," he responded, making no attempt to detain him. "I will send you word as soon as we return."

"Many thanks, and may the favor of the gods guide you," Enecus said, and departed almost at once.

By the time Enecus and Locadio passed through the Porta Nuceria, they needed torches to light their way. "What will it be like if this continues?" Granius asked as he led a heavily laden mule.

"We will have more work than ever before," Locadio answered sharply. "You may be sure of that."

Vibian walked beside them in stoic silence, but his eyes watered continually and there were moments when he faltered. "I do not know that I can walk all the way to Nuceria," he said faintly when they had covered hardly more than a quarter of the distance.

"You must," Locadio told him. "There is no place on the mule."

The road was crowded, but not as much as Enecus had feared. Many Pompeiians were getting beyond the city walls, but most of the population was determined to remain. Ahead of Locadio and Enecus, a scissors grinder and an oculist walked together, trading anecdotes about their customers. The oculist had a wheezing cough but a ready smile, and he seemed to regard the whole situation as a bad comedy.

"How long do you think it will be until we can come back?" Enecus asked. The question had weighed on him all morning, and now he could not hold it inside.

"That is for Vesuvius to determine. I will say this"— Locadio paused to cough—"that if there is another week of this smoke, no one will be able to remain in the city. It will be too unhealthy."

Behind them, Vibian made a terse comment that caused Granius to demand he repeat it. "I only mentioned that an eruption would be welcome. It would end the doubts."

"And other things as well," Granius said.

Locadio shrugged. "The volcano has always vented to the north, away from Pompeii. But you're right, Vibian; at least the waiting would be over." He coughed again, this time so deeply that the others had to stop at the side of the road.

"You're ill," Enecus declared. "The smoke has penetrated your lungs."

Locadio shook his head several times, but he could not stand upright or breathe normally without renewed coughing. "I'll be all right in a moment," he said when he could draw enough air to speak.

"You must rest," Enecus insisted. "If I had a patient at the infirmary in your condition, you would tell me that he had to rest. Wouldn't you?"

"That's different," Locadio grated. His eyes were watering and his face had turned a leaden shade under the smudges of volcanic ash.

"Because you are a physician? You must rest, Locadio, or you will be worse in an hour, and then what? We cannot tend you properly here at the side of the road. It's ridiculous." Enecus motioned to Granius. "Look ahead and see if there are any houses nearby where we might stop for a short while."

173

"Don't you give my slave orders!" Locadio gasped. "Granius. You get...you get..." He gagged, then coughed again.

"I will look," Granius said, unable to conceal his alarm.

He was gone a short while, and when he came back, he looked grave. "No one on this side of the road will take in anyone, not for most of the way to Nuceria."

Enecus cursed. "We must get him inside and give him honeyed herbs. He must not go on like this."

Locadio, who was still bent over, glared up at his apprentice. "You're exceeding your authority, young man."

"You taught me, Locadio, and you told me that I must not let my patients override my good judgment." He motioned to Granius. "We'll have to get him on the mule. Give me two of the packs to carry, and you take two, and there will be room."

"What about him?" Granius asked, nodding toward Vibian.

"He's almost as badly off as Locadio," Enecus pointed out. "There's no good giving him a greater burden than carrying himself. Hurry." As he helped Granius take the packs from the mule's back, he was distracted by a fragment of a memory at the back of his mind. "What is it about the Via Nuceria?" he asked aloud when the question annoyed him enough.

"It's too crowded," Granius panted as he lugged the largest of the packs off the animal.

"No, there's something else. Something about a

villa..." He shook his head. "I wish I could remember. It will be midday soon, and we're not as far along as we ought to be."

"Don't remind me," Granius burst out. "And how are we to know when it's midday when you can hardly see those willows, let alone the sun? If it were up to me, I tell you—"

"Willows!" Enecus shouted. "That's it!"

"What are you talking about?" Granius grumbled, annoyed at having his griping interrupted.

"I remembered. The Villa Salicia. And the man's name was...Niceta. Horatius Ni— No, Hyppolytys Niceta." He let himself smile. "Is there a villa on that side of the road?"

"I didn't look," Granius admitted. "There's nothing on this side."

"I *know* that," Enecus said, then bent toward Locadio. "I think we may have found a place."

"Getting on to Nuceria would be better," Locadio growled.

"Don't you remember that patient of mine, the merchant with the congestion of cold blood? I treated him with foxglove and citrus peel? You recall him?" He had no idea if the portly merchant would be in his villa or had fled with many of the others, but he took hope from the circumstances. "He said I would always be welcome at his villa."

"Patients say that," Locadio said. "That doesn't mean anything to them a week later, and...it was...more than a..." He could not continue to speak.

175

"Granius!" Enecus called. "Go across the road and see if that is the Villa Salicia of Hyppolytys Niceta. Tell him that the physician Locadio Priscus and his apprentice Enecus Cano need room."

Granius hesitated, but Locadio looked balefully at his slave. "Do as Enecus tells you."

Granius needed no more encouragement; he threaded his way through the traffic on the road and was quickly lost in the enveloping darkness.

"How do you feel?" Enecus asked Locadio as an oxen-drawn cart lumbered by them, the two yoked cattle lowing with distress.

"Not well," Locadio admitted at last. "I feel as if my lungs were filled with hot sand." He tried to sigh and could not. "How's Vibian?"

"Better than you," Enecus said, not certain it was so.

"Well, that's something." Locadio lapsed into silence and said nothing until some little time later when Granius reappeared, half running. "Well?"

"The Villa Salicia is five hundred paces farther along the road. That merchant is still there, and he is willing to take us in." The slave beamed with satisfaction.

"Excellent. Get Locadio onto the mule and we'll be off again. Vibian, you hold on to the saddle. It will help you walk." Enecus got his shoulder under Locadio's arm and lifted him to his feet. "It will not be long."

The donkey began to bray with irritation and fear. Vibian went to hold its head while Granius and Enecus struggled to get Locadio aboard, dodging the occa-

176

sional kicks of the creature. When at last Locadio was in the saddle and held there by a length of rope around his waist, they set out again, Granius leading the way and finding them space to pass through the other parties on the road.

Hyppolytys Niceta, a bit leaner than before and more opulently dressed, waited for them at the portico of his villa. "There you are. Come on, come on!" He gestured broadly to the four bedraggled, ash-covered men. "The slaves are waiting to tend to you. Hasn't this been a dreadful time?" He bustled around the donkey, handling the animal with great skill. "Don't frighten the beast, it only makes them more stubborn. You must be firm." He took the bridle and held it steadily while Granius and Enecus got Locadio out of the saddle.

The ground shook and the mountain gave a muffled roar; the donkey tried to rear, his eyes rolling in fright.

"Be quick there," Hyppolytys advised. "The poor creature is half mad."

Locadio stumbled as he set foot on the ground and looked around. "There are more tremors," he said belligerently.

"There are," Enecus agreed, and helped the older man over the threshold of the villa.

Then the ground lurched, and there was a tremendous explosion, a sound so enormous that it battered the world like a hurricane's winds. The darkness was lanced with a frightful spray of light coming from the crest of Vesuvius, and a gigantic cloud, much the shape of a soft round pillow, soared into the sky, hideously lit by the brilliant cascades of fire that now fountained from the mouth of Vesuvius. Then, with one unimaginable surge, the volcano seemed to lift itself, so delicately, as lava emerged and spilled over the cone, sliding down the southern front of Vesuvius.

# XIV

For close to an hour, cinders and ash fell on the Villa Salicia, and occasionally a smoldering rock or boulder would thud onto the tiled roof. The noise of the eruption continued, the thunder of it drumming on the air, making buildings shudder and animals shriek.

"We will put out all the dining couches, that should be some help with those who are hurt." Hyppolytys had to shout to be heard, though Enecus was little more than an arm's length away from him.

"Good!" Enecus yelled back. "Granius will prepare the supplies I have with me. Just be certain that someone stays with my teacher. He is not well, and could suffer from the loss of air at any time. If that should happen, I must attend to him at once, or . . . he might die."

"You tended well enough to me," Hyppolytys said, then bellowed for a slave. "There will be injured on the road, and those who have remained in Pompeii might be trying to leave now. If there are those in need of help, bring them here." He gave the man a pat on the back. "Tie a pillow to your head. That way, you will not be hurt when the rocks fall."

The slave looked terrified, but he nodded in a vague way and started toward the entrance to the villa. Hyppolytys called after him. "Be careful of desperate men, Telos. We are not prepared to fend them off."

When the slave was gone, Enecus asked if there were braziers that could be set up in the vestibule where the couches were.

"Why? We're sure to have more than enough heat," Hyppolytys remarked with an attempt at humor.

"I must boil my tools with astringent herbs," Enecus said. "And quickly."

"Very well."

By the time the braziers were prepared, Telos had brought back the first of the casualties: a man and boy who had been hit by a rain of red-hot lava pebbles.

Enecus had a brief look at them, calling for Granius as he did, then set to work to trim away the burned and broken skin so that he could properly salve the wounds once each had been cleaned. "Give them wine with syrup of poppies," he ordered Granius. "We are going to need a lot of it before this day is through, and we will be able to stretch it if we mix it with wine."

Granius obeyed, but he told Enecus he dreaded what they would see by the end of the day.

"So do I," the young physician admitted. "Hurry up with the drink for them, and be sure that we have an ointment of pansy and willow. At least we're not as likely to run out of that."

"What if the lava comes this way?" Granius could not keep from asking.

"If that happens, we will retreat. If it does not, we will remain where we are until we can go on. Now hurry."

By the time Enecus was half finished with his first patients, Telos had brought him five more, suffering from similar burns. "There are many coming, physician," he warned Enecus and went back to his post on the road.

"I know," Enecus whispered as he continued to stitch closed the pitted and bleeding wounds in the man's shoulders. "Granius! Malachite!"

Granius hurried to obey, but said as quietly as he dared in the wash of sound that continued to issue from the volcano, "We haven't very much of the powdered malachite, master, and we're not likely to get more while we're here."

Enecus kept working, but his heart sank. "All right. Use an admixture of myrrh and ground laurel leaves. It won't be quite as effective, but it's better than nothing. And better than running out."

Hyppolytys came into the room again. "I have in-

structed my slaves to make food for you and the patients, and to see that it is served. Is there anything
that will be better for them than not?"

Enecus finished the suturing, then said, "Hearty,
simple broths are best, and fruit pulps mixed with the
juices can do some good. Do you have much of a
staff here?" Until that moment, he had not thought of
how many might be available to him.

"I sent most of them to Nuceria yesterday evening,
but I have nine slaves in the house and another four
in the stables. If there is anything they might do to
assist you, you have only to ask." He looked at the
stitching in the man's shoulder and nodded. "Very
neat."

"I hope that I will keep on that way. Is there anything
we can do about the stench of this place?" He had
tried to ignore the vile air, but it was becoming more
difficult.

"It's Vesuvius. Sulfur and gases, at the least of it.
Who is to say what else that cursed mountain will have
in store for us." He shrugged. "In the braziers I can
have them burn spices, if that is your wish, but otherwise, there is nothing I can think of." He looked up
as Telos came back into the room, bringing more
patients, these in considerably worse shape than the
first had been. "I will leave you to your tasks."

Enecus had no opportunity to thank Hyppolytys,
and when it occurred to him that he should have done
so, he was trying to keep a middle-aged woman whose
face had been scalded by steam from clawing the skin

off her face. He decided he would have to say it later, when he had time. "Granius! Bring wine here, and give her some while I take care of that boy. His leg is badly hurt." He left Granius to administer the wine while he went to the child. Boiling mud had fallen on his leg, and the hideous stuff had done a great deal of damage, searing away skin and muscle. Enecus ground his teeth at the sight and shouted to Hyppolytys, "Find me your most intelligent slave, providing he has a strong stomach. I need someone to size up the wounded as they arrive and determine which are most in need of aid."

Hyppolytys hurried up to Enecus. "Will I do?"

Enecus stared at him. "You?"

"Do you doubt my judgment?" he asked, but not in any impolite way.

"But you . . . you have done more than enough as it is." Enecus stared down at the boy. "I must have Granius to assist me. There is nothing I can do for this child but amputate the leg, and I cannot do it alone." He had never performed an amputation of more than a finger by himself, and as he said the words, he had to swallow hard. "He will die if I don't . . . he may still die, but he will have a chance."

"Then I will send Granius to you. And I will speak to the wounded coming in. Do you think it will get worse?" He held up his hand. "No, you need not speak. Of course it will get worse."

"Is my teacher . . . ?" Enecus remembered to ask.

"He is resting and there is someone with him, an

183

old nurse. She will not be lax, I promise you." He looked down at the pale child. "To your work, then."

"I'm sorry to— We are ruining your beautiful villa." It was the only thing Enecus could think to say in appreciation.

"Better a ruined villa than ruined lives," the merchant said, and he went to Granius to pass on Enecus' instructions.

Before he had completed the amputation, Enecus saw his first victim of the advancing lava, a young man with his body burned raw over most of one side and part of the other. He could not leave the boy before tying off the blood vessels and cauterizing the stump. "Granius," he ordered hoarsely, "I can finish here without you. Tend to that man." He cocked his head toward the burned man, who was almost mad with pain. "Give him syrup of poppies, undiluted. Half a cup."

Granius stared. "So much?"

"Look at him!" Enecus shouted. "Look at his body! By the gods, don't make him endure more pain!" He signaled to one of the slaves who stood as far away from the dreadful sight in the vestibule as he dared. "Quick! Cauterizing irons. Granius, tend to that poor wretch! Now!"

Granius stumbled off to do as Enecus ordered, and the slave brought the irons, holding them gingerly. As Enecus cauterized the wound, he had to pause to blot the sweat that threatened to run into his eyes. "I will need another tunica. Get one."

The slave gratefully hurried away to comply with his order.

As soon as he had the boy resting on the dining couch, Enecus went to the burned man and looked down at him. "There is so little I can do," he said, and the admission was heartbreaking to him. "Granius, when he has become calmer, put cloths soaked in tincture of aconite on the burns. It might help a little."

Granius wisely did not question these instructions but said, "The master of the house has sent the less badly injured into another room, so that you will have more space to work in."

"Fine. Fine." He looked at the next couch, where a carter sat stoically, trying not to look at the scorched flesh of his forearms and his blistered hands. "I will take care of this man, and then ... Hyppolytys said there was a woman, a potter—where is she?" She had been pointed out to him some little while before.

"She's ... not here," Granius told him after a moment.

"Dead?" Enecus asked.

"Yes."

"If I had been faster ..." He rubbed his face with his hands, then looked automatically for a basin to wash in.

"It would not have mattered," Granius said. "She would not have lived. She was bleeding too badly."

The slave brought Enecus another tunica, the second that hour, and held it out while Enecus stripped off the stained garment he wore and cleaned his hands and face. "There are ten more set out for you, master," he said as he accepted the bloodied tunica. "You have only to ask for them."

There were now over forty people lying in the vestibule, and every couch, chair, and bench in the villa had been pressed into service, though they were still not sufficient. Enecus looked in dismay about him. Not one person in the room required less than immediate attention, and yet he could not deal with more than one at a time. He gritted his teeth and chose the oldest man he saw, whose ashen skin warned the young physician that he was in danger of lapsing into a coma. As he inspected the lacerations on the side of his balding head, Enecus heard Telos bring yet another group into the room. It was all Enecus could do to keep from being overwhelmed by despair. He blotted out his feelings and went to work on the old man.

Sometime later, the slaves brought more torches, and the room took on a lurid glow, as sinister as the continuing brightness of the spreading lava. Enecus muttered brusque thanks to them and kept on working. He was vaguely aware that he had a headache, but it was so minor compared to the devastation of bodies and lives that he saw all around him that he convinced himself it was trivial, and kept on with his work.

"You must eat, master," Granius said to Enecus when he had finished placing the fibulae in a young woman's scalp.

"I haven't the time," Enecus snapped.

"If you do not eat, you will grow faint and will not be able to help these people," Granius pointed out.

"But look at them; they're suffering. I have to act quickly. They are so many and I . . . am without help." Enecus fought back tears, then drew a deep breath. "Yes. All right. But be quick about it. I will attend to that little girl there," he went on, starting toward the child. "She will have to have the aconite cloths, too. Her left arm and most of her back are badly, badly burned." He knew that he had a chance to save this child, for her burns, although severe, covered less than a quarter of her body. There had been others, far worse, for whom he could do nothing. He was not certain he could keep his food down, and he knew he must have a moment of respite if he wished to be able to continue his work. "Granius, I am going to check on Locadio."

"Good lad," Hyppolytys said when Enecus explained what he intended to do. "He was asking for you, around sunset."

"Sunset?" Enecus repeated, surprised. The day had been so dark and his time so filled that he had lost track of time.

"That is the reason for the torches. Go on. My slaves will bring you food to share with your teacher." He gave Enecus an encouraging gesture and gently pointed him out of the vestibule toward the room where Locadio lay.

The nurse was middle-aged and wore her slave's collar like jewelry. She watched Locadio, who dozed fitfully, with care but not with anxiety. "You're the young physician," she said as Enecus came into the room.

"Yes. I . . ." Now that he was there he did not know what to say.

"It is very dedicated of you to spare time for him, and entirely proper," she said, saving him from the embarrassment and confusion that threatened to overwhelm him. "He will be eased by your visit." She reached over the bed and gave Locadio's shoulder a gentle shake.

"Don't be at me, woman!" Locadio grated. "I'm awake."

The nurse ignored this outburst. "Your young associate has come to see you. Can you speak with him? Would you like me to leave?"

Whatever retort was on Locadio's tongue, he held it back. Calmly and with more consideration than he had shown previously, he said, "Thank you for waking me. You may stay if you like." His voice was weak, but he did not cough as he had done before. "You need not look at me that way," he continued with more asperity as he met Enecus' eyes. "I know I have a fever. Even if I were able, I could not help you and would only transmit the illness to your patients."

Enecus was only able to nod. "Are you improving?"

"I will, when it is cooler and that not-to-be-sufficiently-cursed volcano stops making the sewers smell sweet." He had to pause to draw breath, and shot a hasty, annoyed look at the nurse, who had moved to adjust the sheet that covered him.

188

"Yes," Enecus said vaguely.

Locadio's shrewd eyes sized up his apprentice. "Is it bad?"

"Worse than you can imagine," he said with anguish. "And for every one that Telos brings, there are hundreds, far more badly hurt than . . . " Abruptly he sat on the end of the bed. "Don't tell me about life with the Legions, Locadio. I could not bear it."

"No, young man, I won't," Locadio said. "I have been tormenting myself trying to think of a way to aid you, but as I am, I would be another liability, not only to you but to the patients." He pounded his fist ineffectively on the bed. "I could not hold fibulae steady as I am now."

Enecus turned as Locadio began to cough again. "I did not mean . . . Locadio!"

The older man waved him away and motioned for the nurse. "The elixir," he managed to get out.

But the nurse had anticipated him and held out a cup at once. "Here. Drink it quickly." She stood over him as he obeyed.

"Wonderful woman," Locadio wheezed when the worst of his spasm had passed. "Has the heart of a veteran centurion."

This jibe seemed very funny to Enecus, and he laughed, a bit too long and too loudly. "Poor nurse, to have such a child as you in her charge," he said as his laughter ceased.

One of the household slaves came into the room bearing a tray with four platters on it. There was broiled

189

chicken—the sight of it made Enecus worry about his family once more, though they had not crossed his mind more than once or twice since the eruption began—a mixture of chopped figs and dates, vegetables in a spicy sauce, and a mound of small fluffy breads coated with cinnamon and honey. "My master sends you this. We also have broth for you, if it is wanted."

"Bring it for the patient," Enecus said without thinking.

"The gall!" Locadio protested, but dismissed the slave with a gesture and a request that he bring the broth. "Enough for all of us. My apprentice has as much need of it as I do."

They ate in silence; Enecus discovered that he was famished, but Locadio only picked at the food. He chewed very slowly and once looked up at the nurse. "Is there any mint growing near here that is not under a handful of soot?"

"Yes," she said with faint amusement.

"Pick some and have it cooked in this broth with peelings from the inner part of willow bark. Make a lot of it. I am not the only one who will benefit from it." He then ignored the woman as she left the room.

"How are you? Truly," Enecus said when they were alone.

"Not well," Locadio answered. "I fear I will damage my lungs if this keeps on. I try to rest, but with Vesuvius and my own shame at failing my duty, sleep does not bring the alleviation of sorrow it is supposed to."

190

"Do you want a sleeping compound? We are low on syrup of poppies—very low—but if you require some, I will have Granius dilute it in wine and—"

"No. The broth will help." He indicated the remains of the meal. "You'd best finish up, Enecus. You have much more to do."

Sometime very late in the night, Enecus sent Granius to have a rest, and about sunrise, Hyppolytys told Enecus that he would have to get some sleep if he was to go on. Enecus sent them both off with hardly a thought and continued to work on the casualties that continued to arrive. Telos went to bed and was replaced by a stalwart young groom from Alexandria who took up his tasks with such good sense that Enecus asked him what he did, and was informed that the slave cared for the health of the horses in the stable.

The injured continued to come, and for a time they were more badly hurt. As soon as Telos was able to continue, Enecus had the young Alexandrian groom assist him with the more difficult cases, and where there were less terrible problems—a broken leg, singed skin—he left them to the Alexandrian groom, whose name was Bricinus.

By sunset, a century of Legionnaires reached the Villa Salicia. A burly tribune entered the vestibule and turned pale. He looked over his shoulder, shouting for the company's two physicians to come at once. "Who is in charge here!" he demanded in a loud, rough voice.

Hyppolytys stepped forward. "I am Hyppolytys Niceta, a merchant. This is my villa. You are most welcome here."

"How many injured do you have?" the tribune asked. He had recovered himself a little. "And how many physicians?"

"Well, there are two in the villa—" Hyppolytys began.

"Two? For so many?"

"—but one is ill," he finished, ignoring the interruption. "The young man over there, with the red hair, has been the one attending to those who have come here." He gave a fatalistic lift to his shoulders. "Most of the rooms of the villa are filled with injured."

"How many?" the tribune asked again.

Hyppolytys opened his hands. "Three, four hundred. I have not kept count. My slaves may know. I thought it was more important to aid them than count them."

The tribune looked around the room again. "Probably," he said. "We've found few like you, merchant, who took in these unfortunates."

Although he said nothing in response, a strange expression flickered over Hyppolytys' worn features.

"We will be relieving that young physician within the hour. Inform him. We will not move any soldiers into your villa—there is more than enough space at the villa just across the road." He took a last glance around the room. "Just that one young man?"

"We helped, but he has been the only physician," Hyppolytys said. "He is a courageous youth."

"I wish we had twenty more like him right now," the tribune said with feeling, then saluted and left.

Two hours later, after a meal and a quick bath, Enecus went to bed. It was the first sleep he had had in more than thirty-six hours. For the next twelve, he hardly stirred.

 XV

Telos pulled the chariot to the side of the road. "There is the tavern, but it looks filled to me," he said, pointing to the building not far ahead of them.

"The tribune said there would be space for us," Locadio reminded him. "Your master has been more generous than we had any right to hope for, and it is time we no longer trespass on his goodwill." It sounded stiff, even to him, but it expressed his sentiments.

"As you wish. If you find there is not room enough, you may always return to the Villa Salicia," he said, holding the horses firmly.

All Nuceria was filled with people, many living in tents, others simply wandering the streets. Vibian, helping Locadio to get down from the chariot, looked dismayed at the prospect of searching for three women among so many. He accepted the small bag of clothing and another satchel, this one containing the physician's tools and all that was left of their supplies. "I will go to the tavern and be sure that the rooms are ready."

Locadio waited while Granius and then Enecus got out of the chariot. "Thank you, Telos," he called up to the slave, and tossed him a denarius. "You deserve more, but we have little enough to spare."

Telos caught the coin and smiled. "You are very kind, physician. You owe me nothing, but I will take this. Since my master has promised me my freedom, I'm glad of any coins that come my way." He extended his arm in salute, then wheeled the chariot around and started back down the road.

"There are rooms, master," Vibian said as he came up to Locadio. "They are very small and the whole place is crowded, but the tavern keeper has promised not to disturb you."

"Good. I still need rest." He motioned to Enecus, who had been strangely silent for most of the day. "Does this meet with your approval, young man?"

"Whatever suits you," he said distantly.

Locadio put his hand on Enecus' shoulder. "You need more time to rest."

"I've slept more in the last two days than at any time in my life," he protested with an unhappy laugh.

"I said rest, not sleep," Locadio corrected him sharply. "You have been through a time that . . . that few physicians ever see, and it has taken something from you. Enecus, you will need time to recover. You, in your own way, have been as much injured as your patients."

"But I am alive and my skin is whole," Enecus said bleakly as he started toward the tavern.

"And you must forgive yourself for that," Locadio said as he followed after him, Granius walking beside him in case he should stumble.

It took five days for Enecus to locate his mother and sister. He found them in a large tent on the road between Nuceria and Nola, where they had set up a makeshift thermopolium. Jocanda was tending the grill while Pyralis basted chicken parts.

"How much?" he called out, like the other customers.

"Five coppers for five pieces of chicken in a bread," Pyralis answered without looking up.

"You're getting expensive, little sister," Enecus chided her, and although he could not yet sound as light-hearted as he once had been, he was rewarded with a shriek and a raised head.

"Enecus! *Enecus!* Mother, Enecus is here!" Pyralis screamed and laughed at once. She ducked under the plank that served as a counter and rushed into his arms. "Oh, Enecus. I feared you were ... that you were ..."

He kissed her forehead. "So did I, Pyralis." He could not keep from glancing over his shoulder at the white cone of Vesuvius, shrunken now that the fury of its eruption had blasted away part of its slopes.

"They say that Pompeii is . . . gone," she whispered, suddenly serious, her smile wiped from her face.

Rhea came from behind the tent where she had been making flat breads in a small oven. Her face was wan, but her eyes lit up at the sight of her son. "You are safe," she said, and came to embrace him.

"We have not yet . . . had word from your father," Rhea admitted a little while later while they sat together under a fig tree. They could hear Jocanda arguing with one of the customers, and this familiar disruption was strangely welcome to the three.

"Nor have I," Enecus said. "But I talked to Salvius before I left, and he gave me his word . . ." He thought a moment. "If Salvius got out, I believe that Father did, too." He did not like having to say it that way, for it left too much uncertainty. His reverie was interrupted by a loud cry.

"There he is!"

At first Enecus did not realize that he was the object of this outburst, but then a squat man with bandaged arms rushed toward him. "You are the pride of Apollo himself!" the man bellowed, and seized Enecus in a bear hug that left the young man bewildered and breathless.

"Sir, I do not know you," he said when he could draw breath.

"Do not know me?" the man repeated incredulously. "Listen to him! Modest as well as inspired!" He gestured to a few other people near the tent. "And I

197

suppose you will try to tell me that you do not know them, either." He laughed loudly.

Rhea and Pyralis stared in confusion that bordered on alarm. "What do you want with my son?" Rhea inquired in a manner that usually dampened enthusiasm.

"Your son, is he? Well, I will take this opportunity to tell you, madam, that your son is the sort of physician this Empire should have more of."

Rhea's expression softened at once, and Pyralis' face fairly glowed with curiosity. "What has he done, that you say that?"

"You mean that he hasn't told you?" the stranger cried in disbelief.

Enecus broke into the man's question. "I have just found my mother and sister. There has been no time to say much to them."

"What is it, sir?" Pyralis asked with her most charming smile, which she knew would be enough to get the story out of the stranger.

The man kept one arm around Enecus' shoulder. "You have a wonder here, ladies, and you must be proud of him. Why, if it weren't for him, I and my family would be done crisper than your chicken. That villa, with all the hurt and burned, it was like something after a war. And there was this fine young fellow, calm as you please, going from patient to patient, tending them as if there were nothing to it. He would put his hand on a man and know at once what was to be done. And there was Vesuvius belching out fire and ruin be-

198

hind him and the whole place smelling worse than a fishmonger's dung heap on a July afternoon. Not that you could tell it from him." He chuckled merrily.

"Enecus?" Rhea said, turning pale. "Did you?"

"I wouldn't say I was calm, just worn to numbness. And as to knowing what to do, I did as best I could, given where we were and what was at hand—which was precious little." He flushed. "You are kind, sir, and I thank you for what you say, but you exaggerate. If you must be grateful to someone, be grateful to Hyppolytys Niceta, whose villa that is."

"Oh, of course," the man said, dismissing the matter. "But an open villa with no one to aid becomes a house of the dead very shortly." He bowed to Rhea and Pyralis. "You are fortunate, both of you. I count it an honor to have this chance to speak to you. Well." He rounded on Enecus again. "May the gods favor you all your life long, physician. If anyone deserves it, you do."

When the man had bustled off, Enecus looked at his mother and sister. "It wasn't like that," he said. Then, slowly at first, the story came out of him. Somewhere in the middle, while he was speaking of a child who had been brought to him—"And there was nothing I could do for the little girl, nothing; much of her skin was gone and what she had left was broken and blistered. She was already sunk into coma and her eyes gave no response to light"—he began to cry, silently for a time, and then in sobs that wrenched through him. When he tried to apologize to Rhea and

199

Pyralis, they put their arms around him and held him until it was over.

Down the central street of Nuceria came a slave carrying a sign reading:

SALVIUS VALENS
searches for the family of
AMALIUS CANO
and the physician Locadio Priscus

There had been many such signs over the last ten days, and most of them were doomed to frustration at best, grief at worst.

It was Granius who saw the slave, and he went at once to the tavern where Locadio was recuperating from his illness. "Master! Master," he shouted as he burst into the room.

"What is it now, another dancing bear?" Locadio asked testily. "It's bad enough that this place is hot and the baths are overcrowded, but the noise—"

Granius cut into this complaint. "A slave, master, from Salvius Valens! He is looking for Enecus, and for you."

Locadio looked up sharply, his manner entirely altered. "A slave?"

"Yes. You know, with the signs, like the others we've seen." Granius was excited, and as a result he stumbled over the words in his enthusiasm.

"And did you speak to him?" Locadio demanded. "Well?"

"I . . . I wanted to tell you about it," Granius said, some of his delight turning to doubt.

"And now you've told me," Locadio growled. "Why are you not out in the street, stopping that slave and telling him that his task is over? Go on!"

Granius rushed to obey. He ran out of the tavern and into the crowded street. It took him the better part of an hour to locate the slave again, but when he did, he rushed up to the man, panting with exertion and relief. "You!"

The slave did not turn at first, and when he did, it was clear that he did not expect much. "Yes?"

"You're from Salvius Valens? The cloth merchant?"

"Yes, Salvius Valens is my master," the slave said, frowning and puzzled.

"My master is Locadio Priscus, and I know where the wife and children of Amalius Cano are." He smiled, his hands held together in front of him, fingers locked in excitement.

"Where?" the slave asked, his interest sharpened.

"The physician lies in that tavern, recovering from an illness. Cano's family have set up business about three thousand paces down the road to Nola. Enecus spends his afternoons with them, but the rest of the time he is here." He beamed. "If you will come with me—"

"Yes," the slave said, and lowered his sign. "My arms ache from carrying this thing. The pole feels as if it weighs more than a dozen boulders by the end of the day."

"Amalius Cano, is he well?" Granius asked as they threaded their way back toward the tavern.

"He suffered some burns, but he is well. He is with my master on Sicilia. There is a boat waiting at Salernum to carry you to him." He shook his head in amazement. "Who would have thought that they all lived? So many did not, and there are thousands missing; no one knows what became of them."

"Yes," Granius said, turning serious once more. "And who can reckon the cost of that?"

The slave smiled. "The gods, perhaps."

"Perhaps," Granius said, and stood aside to let the other man enter the tavern ahead of him.

"Who would have thought we'd have so little left?" Locadio asked of the air as he stood near the entrance to the tavern inspecting the baggage he and Enecus had piled there. "So many years in Pompeii, and this is all that is left to show for it." He sighed once, then shook himself, as if to cast off the gloom that held him.

"What was used went to the good of your patients," Enecus said as he put the last bundle on the pile.

"*Your* patients, Enecus. I can take no credit for what you did for those unfortunates." He tried to smile, but his mouth only made a lopsided grimace.

"If you had not taught me, and taught me well, I would have been no use to them or you or . . . anyone." He gave Locadio a long, steady look. "If I helped those people, you are the one they should thank. In a year

202

or two, when I have had more time to become a real physician, then I might say otherwise, but not now, while I am still an apprentice." He braced his hands on his hips, wanting to shake Locadio and rid him of his melancholy.

"Apprentice? You? My good young man, you are as much a physician now as I can make you. Years will do the rest, and whatever life sends you." He motioned to Granius. "Tell the slave that we are ready to leave when he is."

Enecus reached out and touched Locadio's arm. "You may think that, but I don't. For a day or two, when the world was coming apart, perhaps then I was enough of a physician because it was necessary, but to do what you have done so long, caring for those who come to you, day after day, I have not learned enough to do that with skill or with . . . with tact, I suppose." It was difficult for him to admit this, and saying the words made him painfully aware of how true they were.

"Nor have I," Locadio said, refusing to look at Enecus. "The slaves will carry the baggage, but Enecus, I . . ."

Granius approached them, a self-conscious smirk on his features. "I've found a cart and one of those big Asian hounds to pull it. We'll get it loaded and be off." He turned from Locadio to Enecus, expecting praise.

"Good," Enecus said when Locadio remained silent. "I know we'll all be glad of it."

Belatedly, Locadio agreed. "Yes. You did well, Granius." He put his hands to his temples. "My head still aches. I wish we had that tincture of pansy and willow with us."

"Do you want me to try to find some? There must be an herb seller in the forum. It won't take long." Enecus was baffled by this lethargy that had taken hold of Locadio and stubbornly refused to end. "What is it?"

For once Locadio did not pretend to misunderstand. He took a deep breath, as if he had been running hard. "I suppose now that you'll be starting out on your own, Salvius will be willing to set you up in practice somewhere, no doubt."

"Possibly, but . . ." Enecus frowned as his words trailed off. "What are you going to do?"

"Oh, I don't know. Find a man with a couple of hundred slaves and take a contract to keep them well for a year or two. That should pay enough to let me start a practice somewhere, in time."

Enecus could not keep the pain from his face. "And where do I—do you want to continue as my master?"

"You don't need a master; I've already told you that. Besides, what have I to offer now that would be worth the cost of apprenticeship? I agreed to instruct you for three years." Again he sighed. "Your father can't fault me for the interruption."

"No," Enecus replied tersely. He could think of nothing more to say, but he could not simply leave Locadio. "If you will not have me as an apprentice, will you have me as an assistant?"

204

Locadio looked toward him at last. "Not as an assistant, no."

It was Enecus' turn to sigh. "All right."

For the first time since Vesuvius belched out destruction to their city, Locadio smiled. "I *will* have you for a partner, if you are amenable."

Enecus' sudden grin said more than any words could just how agreeable he was. "You won't regret it, Locadio, I promise you."

"I know that. I only hope that *you* will not regret it." He said the last in his familiar gruff manner, folding his arms and trying to look severe while gratitude and friendship shone in his eyes.

Though the terrace of the Valens villa faced the Mare Tyrrhenum and Neapolis on the distant shore, all those seated there to enjoy the evening looked away from the view because of the distant, ash-white cone of Vesuvius.

"Will you stay in Panormus, Salvius?" Enecus asked his friend as slaves filled the wine cups for the guests.

"For the time being. Eventually I suppose I will have to go to Roma. That is the best place for me now. I might decide to make a home in Ostia, to be closer to the docks and the shipping." He paused sadly for a moment. "I wish my father had been able to get away from Pompeii. I miss him more than I ever..."

"But you said that he was aboard his ship...I thought—" Enecus began, and was grateful when Salvius interrupted him.

"He made it to his ship—oh, yes. But the mud that came before the lava was not far behind, and it heated the water in the bay so that the caulking on the seams of the ship grew soft, and water rushed in, boiling water." He drank deeply. "It happened to so many."

"I am sorry," Enecus said most sincerely. He wished there were more he could say to give Salvius comfort, but the words he thought of seemed so empty.

Amalius shifted on his couch, trying to find a position in which his just-healing skin did not sting or itch. "Your father was a good man, Salvius, and a credit to his profession and his city. You have every reason to honor his memory."

"Yes," Salvius said quietly. "And yet I would so much rather honor *him*."

There was little that anyone could say to this, and an awkward silence fell.

"You're freeing Granius?" Salvius asked Locadio a bit later. "Enecus mentioned that sometime today."

"Oh, yes," Locadio answered, relieved that the subject was changed. "After all he has done, it would be a shame for me if I should keep him in a collar. He has agreed to stay on with me, at least for a year and a day. What arrangements come then, well, that is up to the gods."

"Then you will want to have a celebration for him," Salvius said. "It would please me if you were to have it here."

"Only if I am permitted to supply the food," Pyralis said, and then a look of distress crossed her face. "I don't know when I will have the chance to cook again, or to serve all the dishes that . . . everyone liked so much . . . before." She wiped her eyes impatiently. "I thought I'd stopped doing this," she said by way of excusing herself.

"It will take more than a week or two," Locadio pointed out with more kindness than he usually showed to those near him. "For many of them . . . of *us*, as well, it may be the task of a lifetime." He stared down into his cup. "It can't be undone, and what has been lost cannot be recovered. Still, if we let catastrophe rule our lives, then we are one with those buried in Pompeii and Herculaneum, and the mountain has victims enough already."

"But the thermopolium is gone, and everything in it. What have we to start with but a few recipes remembered and ten gold coins?" Pyralis sounded more distressed now, but her face was calmer. She looked toward her father and mother, then at Enecus. "Your partnership . . ."

"You still have your talents," Locadio pointed out.

"But unlike you," she countered, "I need more than a patient and a handful of herbs to have a business."

Amalius was shocked at his daughter's attitude. "Pyralis!"

"She's right," Enecus said, silencing the others. "A physician does not need to have food and wine around him to practice, but both of us need a handful of herbs. She cannot begin as a street vendor if she wishes to have her tratorium one day; it would take too long and cost too much." He stared at Salvius. "You offered to

lend me the money to start a practice with Locadio—
would you lend it to my sister instead?"

This time both Amalius and Rhea protested, and
Locadio demanded to be told what this was supposed
to mean.

"I offered to lend Enecus enough money to start an
infirmary, that's all," Salvius said, thinking to put an
end to the dissension around him; as soon as he had
spoken, he was assailed with questions.

"A fine thing, my apprentice taking money on my
behalf!" Locadio muttered.

"What do you mean, asking for money for this family?" Amalius exclaimed at the same time.

"I'll borrow my own money!" Pyralis shouted.

"Oh, for the patience of Saturn," Enecus said in
vexation. "How are we supposed to survive, without
the aid of our friends? Salvius *offered* the money; I did
not ask him for it. Who better to take it from than a
man who knows the worth of you, Pyralis, and you,
my parents, and you, my teacher? What person would
you rather have it from? We have been friends for ten
years. We were boys together!" At this outburst, Enecus felt a deep sadness as he realized that he and
Salvius were boys no longer.

Apparently Salvius shared this sense, for he came
across the terrace and put his hand on Enecus' shoulder. "It was less than two years ago that we chose our
careers. Who would have thought this would come of
it?"

Enecus nodded. "It's gone, that time."

"Yes, except from our memories." He cleared his

208

throat. "Better to have help from me than from strangers. We are Pompeiians, after all."

That grim reminder touched them all. Enecus looked at his sister. "Think of that, Pyralis. You know you will repay as soon as you can, and so does Salvius."

"I am not a poor man," Salvius said modestly. "Let me do this to honor my father, and our lost city, and you will give me satisfaction. All of you." He signaled for more wine. "The evening meal is almost ready. Let me propose this to you: enough money to found your tratorium, Pyralis, and your infirmary, Locadio, with the understanding that every six months I will expect a sum of not less than ten percent of the loan, until it is paid. If for some reason it is not possible for you to do this, I will become your partner and that will settle the matter entirely."

There was an embarrassed quiet on the terrace.

"I *do* need money for the tratorium," Pyralis admitted. "Father, let me tell him we agree, so that we may go on as we did before. If we don't do this, we will have to sell Jocanda in order to purchase a thermopolium, and that would be a very bad trade." She looked toward Salvius before her father could speak. "I will welcome you as a partner from the first, if that is your preference."

Salvius grinned. "No, I think my wife would object. She is very specific about my ventures, since her fortune is invested in the spice trade as well as in cloth and dyes. She does not like to see our interests too scattered. I will make you the loan and we will see how it goes. Who knows? She may come to like the notion of having a partnership with someone who serves very good food."

Enecus met Salvius' gaze frankly. "Thank you."

"Thank me when a year is over and I've had my payments or my partnerships," he said with a gesture to show that he did not want to be thanked anymore. "What about you, then? Have you decided where you want to open this infirmary of yours?"

"Locadio and I discussed that this afternoon," Enecus replied slowly. "Now that we're going to be partners."

"And? Would you like to stay on in Sicilia?" It was apparent that this was what he was hoping, and so Enecus was all the more troubled that he had to disappoint him. "There are volcanoes on this island. I don't think I want to live close to one again. I would never see a bit of smoke or smell sulfur that I would not think the world was ending again. No," he went on, deliberately trying to sound more optimistic, "Locadio has a niece in Graviscae who has half an insula standing empty. With a little persuasion, she might well permit us to open our infirmary there."

"Graviscae is between Ostia and Pisae, isn't it?" Salvius asked. "That would not be too bad. I have merchants in both Ostia and Pisae. We will be able to visit often." He looked at the others. "Are you all going to Graviscae as well?"

"No," Pyralis said, sounding forlorn once more. "We talked it over and decided that it would be best to find a port city where there are many people and where good food is especially valued. Brundisium might be

210

the best, next to Ostia, and there would not be quite so much competition, or so many from Pompeii trying to make a new start. Brundisium is on the Greek shipping lanes, and my mother is Greek, remember."

"Brundisium," Salvius repeated. "A good choice, I suppose."

The realization that they were to be separated settled over the group on the terrace like a sodden mantle. Finally Locadio spoke up.

"Well, this gives us reason to travel, Enecus. Brundisium is an interesting place, and it would do both of us good to take a little time every year to get away so that we do not become too worn out or jaded."

Amalius' face brightened. "Yes, that would be wise, wouldn't it?"

Salvius grinned. "I know I ought to be infuriated that you are all going to leave me, but . . . but I am so overjoyed that you are alive that it does not matter if you are in Sicilia or Gallia or Gaza, so long as you are living." He turned his head as a gong sounded from inside the villa. "The slaves are bringing supper."

"Wonderful," Rhea said, then looked at her daughter. "I know how you love to cook, Pyralis, but by the time you reach my age, you will be delighted to let others take over the task every now and then."

Locadio and Amalius went in through the open door, arm in arm, Locadio taking care that Amalius did not injure himself.

"Well," Salvius said, pausing to speak in private with Enecus. "So it's settled, then."

"I guess it is," Enecus agreed. "You are very generous. Without your help, we would all be in a sorry mess."

Salvius shrugged. "I can't cook a meal more complicated than boiled dates, and you know what becomes of me when others are hurt. But I do know cloth and I have ships and money, and you are my oldest friend."

"Don't be so critical of yourself, Salvius. Aid like this is kindness itself. I'll say it again: you are very generous."

"I am very fortunate," Salvius corrected him with a sigh. "The gods showed me favor and spared my life. I must be deserving of it."

"You *are*. I wish I could convince you of that," Enecus told him.

"Do well with your infirmary, and I will be gratified," Salvius said, trying to dismiss the matter.

Enecus was not to be put off. "Perhaps, one day, I can repay you properly," he said, then added, "And I do not mean in money."

"I know," Salvius concurred.

"And in time I will show you that your confidence in me and my family is not misplaced." Enecus was relieved; just saying the words eased the burden of his gratitude.

Salvius put his arm around his friend's shoulder and deliberately turned so that they faced the cone of Vesuvius and the desolation that swept down from its crest to the twilight-dark sea. "Enecus, you already have."

GLOSSARY

Latin Terms

A (pl. AS): A small coin equal roughly to a half-penny.

ATRIUM: The hall or entrance room in a Roman house.

AUREUS (pl. AUREI): A gold coin, worth about twenty-five denarii, or, in modern terms, between $35.00 and $50.00.

BESTIARIUS (pl. BESTIARII): A person who works with wild animals. The noun is usually found in the plural. This category included stunt-performing horsemen, but not charioteers.

BIGA (pl. BIGAE): An open two-horse chariot, the most common vehicle for day and local use in Roman cities.

BIREME: A boat, sometimes called a galley, with two ranks of oars. Most Roman boats were powered by oars; the sails were used to assist the oarsmen when the wind was at the back of the vessel.

CALDARIUM (pl. CALDARIA): A hot bath, usually taken in small, waist-deep tubs large enough to accommodate four to ten persons.

CENTURION: An officer commanding a century in the Roman army.

213

CENTURY: A unit of the Roman army, originally consisting of 100 troops, or one sixtieth of a legion.

CIMRI: A people now most often called Celts.

DALMATICA (pl. DALMATICAE): One of the two most common garments worn in Imperial Rome. It was loose, made of cotton, linen, or wool, and either knee or ankle length, and was similar to a modern caftan.

DENARIUS (pl. DENARII): A Roman coin, usually made of silver, originally worth ten copper as, but at the time of this book worth about four sesterii, with a modern worth of around $1.25 to $1.60.

EMPORIUM: A warehouse or storage building.

EQUESTRIAN: A social rank above middle class but not necessarily noble. Literally, one entitled to ride a horse in an official procession or ceremony.

FACTION: A racing corporation, one that sponsored chariot races. Factions owned charioteers and horse farms and often paid large amounts of money to improve arenas. The members of the factions were as extreme in their team loyalties as lifelong football or baseball fans are. There were four factions at this time: the Blues, the Reds, the Greens, and the Whites. Faction members often had the color of their faction painted on their tombstones.

FIBULA (pl. FIBULAE): A straight pin, often secured with a ring, similar to a brooch, used in medicine to hold wounds closed. Fibulae were also used to fasten clothes and as ornaments.

FORUM (pl. FORA): A square or plaza, often the location of markets, civic buildings, temples, amphitheaters, or theaters.

FRIGIDARIUM (pl. FRIGIDARIA): Cold bath, usually shallow, often located in the darkest part of a Roman bath complex. A frigidarium usually held no more than six people at a time.

214

INSULA (pl. INSULAE): A block building, sometimes with a court in the center, with shops and businesses on the ground floor and apartments on the floors above. Insulae ranged from luxurious to shoddy and were the most common form of housing available in Pompeii or any other walled Roman city of the time. Building regulations usually limited the height of these buildings to no more than four stories above ground.

MANTELE: A cloth that was worn around the shoulders, similar to a short cape.

MANTILE: A cloth that was tied around the waist, an apron.

MARE TYRRHENUM: The sea to the west of Pompeii.

PALLA: A long and wide outer garment worn by Roman women.

PALLIUM: A garment, originally Greek but adapted by the Romans as summer business wear. It usually hung below the knee, and was belted and slung from one shoulder. It was made of cotton or linen.

PATRICIAN: A member of one of the noble families of the Roman Republic.

PERISTYLE: A court with a colonnade around it.

PRAETOR: In the Great Games, this was the judge, the keeper of the laps, and the umpire for the chariot races.

QUADRAN: A copper coin worth one quarter of an a. The quadran was at that time the most common copper coin in circulation, since it was small and easily carried. Fifteen to sixteen of them made up the value of one sesterius.

QUADRIGA: A four-horse chariot, most often used for chariot racing. If the quadriga was the high-test competition sports car of its day, then the biga was the family car.

SESTERIUS (pl. SESTERII): A coin worth about one quarter of a denarius. Its metal composition varied, but was usually a mix of silver and copper.

STOLA: A long outer garment worn by Roman matrons.

SYNTHESIS: A light upper garment; dressing gown.

TEPIDARIUM (pl. TEPIDARIA): The cool bath, often very large, like a swimming pool. The tepidarium usually adjoined a gymnasium and was a place to socialize as well as take exercise, swim, and have a massage.

THERMOPOLIUM (pl. THERMOPOLIA): A fast-food grill, usually a street-side business specializing in hot foods and wine. A thermopolium offered limited seating, and the quality of the food served ranged from terrible to marvelous.

TOGA: The formal wear of the Roman Empire. It was a cumbersome garment that took great expertise to drape on the wearer. A dressy daytime version of it was shorter, with less cloth, and most often brightly colored, as most Roman garments were.

TRATORIUM (pl. TRATORIA): A café, a step up from a thermopolium. The customers were seated and the food was brought to them. Unlike thermopolia, tratoria offered a wide variety of foods on their menus.

TRIBUNE: Any official of ancient Rome chosen by the common people to protect their rights against the patricians.

TRIREME: A boat with three banks of oars, most often, but not exclusively, military.

TUNICA (pl. TUNICAE): The most popular of Roman garments. Tunicae were knee length, and were worn with or without sleeves. They were made of every fabric available in Rome, and in a tremendous variety of colors. In winter, wool leggings were worn under two or three wool tunicae; in the summer, a very lightweight tunica of linen or cotton was worn.

UVULA (pl. UVULAE): One of the most common Roman medical tools. It was a clamp, often with toothed grips, like pliers, and frequently had a small sharpened area at the end of the handles to aid in cutting away damaged tissue.

VENATION: A beast hunt in the circus or amphitheater.

216

Roman Medicine

ARABIC OIL: Used to treat a number of conditions, but primarily as topical relief for insect bites and to inhale for congestion. The oils most often used were licorice and camphor.

BENDING FEVER: Tetanus.

CANNABIS: Oil of hemp, most often used to treat persistent stress and severe attacks of asthma.

COMPOSER; COMPOSING DRINK: Any of a number of preparations that caused the patient to relax. The herbs used depended often on the reason for the tension.

CRAMP:

SIDE: Most often duodenal ulcers, but also liver disease or other internal problems. Treatment varied, but a light diet was the first suggestion.

HEAD: Sometimes indicative of stroke, or prestroke conditions, although migraine headache and brain tumors were also classified under head cramp prior to any surgery. Treatment varied.

LEG: Where obvious injury was not present, hot-oil massages and the addition of fried cheese to the diet were the usual treatments.

HAND: If there was no sign of arthritis or other joint disease, hand cramps were treated with massage and with alternating hot and cold baths. Where joint disease was present, poultices were applied. A standard poultice for arthritis contained wintergreen, willow bark, and mace.

DISEASE OF THE CRAB: Skin cancer. Sometimes the diseased skin was surgically removed; other times the affected area was treated with poultices and ointments. Cannabis and syrup of poppies were prescribed for pain. The Romans did not regard cancer of the internal organs and skin cancer as the same disease.

DRAWING PASTE: A paste used to draw infection to the surface of a wound.

FALLING SICKNESS: Epilepsy. This was most often treated with an infusion of mistletoe, lavender, myrtle, amber, and pennyroyal, which provide strong antispasmodic agents.

FOXGLOVE: Used in the treatment of heart disease from ancient times to the present day.

HAWTHORN: Used in the treatment of heart disease. The plant contains an anticoagulant.

HIND LIQUID: A tranquilizing liquid made in India. It is an infusion made of mild sedative herbs including either cannabis or belladona, with large amounts of either cinnamon or pepper to act as mild stimulants.

JUNIPER BERRIES: Used as a diuretic and, in the last few hundred years, to flavor gin.

LEMON AND ORANGE PEEL: Used in a variety of treatments. Only the dried peel was available in Pompeii. Citrus peel contains many trace elements and vitamin C.

MALACHITE: A green-colored stone, which when powdered reduced bacteria and infection in wounds.

MANDRAGORA: A powerful antispasmodic and narcotic; the Romans used this plant for a topical anesthetic. It was very rarely used internally.

MORTIFICATION:

INTESTINES: The diagnosis Romans gave for either colitis or appendicitis that resulted in peritonitis. Treatment for colitis usually proved successful; treatment for appendicitis usually did not.

OPEN WOUNDS: Gangrene. High amputation was the only treatment available.

PURGATIVE: Any of a number of treatments to purge the body, that is, to force the body to get rid of harmful substances through vomit, stool, and/or urine.

PUTREFIED: Having infected but not mortified—dead—tis-

218

sue. Often used to indicate the presence of pus.

SPOILED: Having obvious bacterial infection, such as mold on fruit.

SWEET DISEASE: Diabetes. The Romans were aware of the disease and its potential for being fatal. Their usual prescriptions were for a limited diet and the use of purgatives and diuretics. The Romans thought diabetes was an allergy.

SYRUP OF POPPIES: Processed opium, used as an anesthetic.

TAINTED: Having no obvious bacterial infection but nevertheless unsafe, such as meat filled with salmonella.

WHEEZING SICKNESS: Asthma and other bronchial allergies. The most common prescription was a strong potion taken orally containing comfrey, valerian, hyssop, and nettles.

WILLOW BARK: Probably the most common remedy prescribed in Rome—and today as well, for that matter, since the compound it contains is the basic ingredient of aspirin. It was taken as a tea or applied topically in poultices or ointments.